MAKAI UNITED

Tara Fairfield, Ed.D.

ISBN:1537352326
ISBN-13: 978-1537352329

DEDICATION

My deepest appreciate to my family, who encourage and support me every day. They are both critics and cheerleaders, and I love them so much. My grandchildren inspire me to never give up.

Family is the foundation for a life filled with love. I am grateful to God for the overwhelming joy, peace and love he has poured into my life.

ACKNOWLEDGMENTS

A big thank you to Onisha Ellis for entering my readers contest to title this story. She submitted the winning title: Makai United. It really captures the essence of this third, and final, Makai novel.

The cover was designed by the very talented Elizabeth Delana Rosa. Thank you!

CHAPTER 1

TESSA

LA HANAU

BIRTHDAY

"Breathe, Rachel, breathe." I cooed, passing another ice chip to Mike as he wiped Rachel's brow with a cool cloth. Seeing her face contorted in pain twisted my gut. I cast another worried glance over to Kele who calmly worked in the corner laying out blankets over warming stones. Wisps of steam floated in the air, smelling of lavender. "Shouldn't you be doing something to help her?"

Kele edged closer to me and spoke softly, "Dat little kika come soon Tessa, your sistah will be fine, garans."

I frowned at him. Doubts about Rachel and Mike's decision to have the baby in Moku-ola, surrounded by friends, churned in my head. I wondered if we should have insisted she give birth in a traditional hospital. A few pieces of modern medical equipment and MD's with fancy degrees hanging on the wall would be soothing about now. Our city beneath the sea was a marvel to behold. Located within a hidden lava cavern deep in Hawaiian waters, Moku-ola offered a peaceful environment connected to our precious ocean. What it lacked, was extensive medical equipment and staff. Kele was the city's healer and he was very gifted. He had brought many children into the world, but this was my big sister and the thought of anything happening to her paralyzed me. "She doesn't look fine to me Kele.

She's in pain."

Rachel reached out her hand to me. "Sis, don't worry, you're stressing me out. This is the way I wanted it. Just those I love and trust." Her face tensed as another contraction hit and all talk ceased as we waited it out, guilt oozing like sludge over my heart.

As her muscles eased and she pressed back against her pillow, I blurted, "Sorry Rachel. I'll relax, promise."

She smiled weakly before closing her eyes and taking a few deep breaths as Mike massaged her shoulders. He caught my eye and winked before focusing back on my sister.

Kupua clasped my hand and tugged, cocking his head toward the door. With a furtive glance at Rachel, I nodded and allowed him to drag me into the hallway where I vented my frustration. "Why is it taking so long? She's been in labor for hours now, shouldn't the baby be coming? Do you think something's wrong?"

Stroking my palm, he smiled, displaying the dimples I loved. "Tessa, take a deep breath. Rachel and the baby are fine. Kele knows what he's doing. If he thought there was a problem, he would tell us. You know how over protective he can be."

Kele's voice rose from inside the room. "I heard dat brah."

Kupua laughed and shot back. "Good. Now mind your own business. Private conversation happening here, brah."

I inhaled, closed my eyes and released the worry clouding my mind. Tension and stress rolled off my shoulders and I leaned forward, resting my head against Kupua's chest, exhaling in relief.

"Thanks." I raised my head to gaze into his warm eyes. "How do you always know what I need?"

He chuckled. "I pay attention."

Akalei breezed past us balancing a tray piled high with cups of ice. "No dawdling in the hall. The little one will be here anytime now, then the real party begins."

I quirked an eyebrow at Kupua.

He turned me back toward the room and nudged me forward, a hint of humor lacing his words. "You know the city will erupt in celebration once the baby's born. There's no stopping it, Tessa. It's our tradition."

Plodding into the room and rubbing my eyes, I mumbled, "I just don't think I've got much energy left in me to celebrate. We've gotten no sleep."

Rachel let out a spine-curdling scream and my body shot to life, hurdling to her side in a flash. She sat upright, Mike supporting her back and sweat trickling down her face.

Kele shouted. "It's time! One more push an da little one will be here!"

I tensed, holding my breath as Rachel used every last bit of energy to push. Her face contorted in pain. Moments later a shrill cry exploded through the air, accompanied by flailing arms and legs. Kele cradled my new niece against his chest and inspected her thoroughly. Rachel fell back against the pillows, her face relaxed, shining with streams of tears. I reached for her hand, squeezing tight. "She's so beautiful."

Mike's face glowed as he leaned over and kissed Rachel on the forehead. "Awesome job, Rach. We have a daughter." My sister beamed at her husband, her tired smile lighting her face.

Kele wrapped the baby in a light blanket and handed her over to Rachel's outstretched arms, cooing softly. "Dat one cutie, Rachel. She's perfect."

Akalei peered over his shoulder. "What are you going to name her?"

Rachel stroked her daughter's cheek with a finger. "Okalani."

Mike slid onto the bed next to Rachel and laid his head on her shoulder, gazing at his new child with eyes glazed over with love. "It means from heaven. Perfect for her, don't you think?"

I choked back the lump in my throat, my voice cracking. "Yeah, it's perfect, just like her." Little Okalani sported a full head of black hair, dark lashes and round cheeks. Her mouth was a pink rosebud topped by a button nose, a perfect blend of her mother and father. She took my breath away. My sister and her husband wrapped around their new daughter and responsibility settled over my heart with a renewed determination to address the threats to her future.

"We will all keep her safe," I whispered. Akalei and Kele both nodded and edged closer, drawn to this tiny miracle like moths to a flame. I stroked a finger over her silky golden skin and she wiggled in Rachel's arms. "You did good, Rach."

Akalei pressed against my back and reached over my head to squeeze Okalani's toes. "She's so tiny, like a miniature doll."

Okalani turned red and belted out a wail. Rachel snuggled her closer until she calmed. "Nothing miniature about her lungs."

Mike puffed up. "Takes after her dad."

Kele inserted himself between my sister and Okalani's new fan club. "No hassle me. Da lil wahine need to get cleaned up, yeah, no?" He wiped the squirming infant with a moist towel and inspected her eyes, nose and throat. Unwrapping a stethoscope from around his neck, he listened to her heart. "Dat one strong girl." He nodded to Rachel and wiggled out from between us.

Kupua squeezed my shoulder. "Time to announce her arrival to the city. They are all waiting."

I leaned over and planted a kiss on my new niece's forehead. Her skin felt softer than the velvet underbelly of a manta ray. The pure innocent scent of newborn restored my energy. I lingered, before straightening my shoulders and taking Kupua's hand. "Let's get this party started."

CHAPTER 2

TESSA

PA'INA

PARTY

Strands of shells connected torches surrounding the sacred pool. Flames flickered in the slight breeze blowing in from tunnels that fed the main cavern of Moku-ola. The city lay nestled within the carved volcanic rock of a massive cave, with enough room to house the eight hundred residents. Fresh air blew in from volcanic tunnels connecting to the surface, providing breathable oxygen. High above, the ocean swirled across the clear ceiling, like a fluid blue-green cloud. Our very own hidden city beneath the sea.

Small groups of people milled around the pool, subdued and waiting for our news, their faces expectant and hopeful. Children splashed in the tide pools scattered along paths, giggling in hushed voices for fear their parents might squash their play.

Holding hands, Kupua and I stepped onto the glass platform directly over the water of the sacred pool which fed directly into the ocean. Voices hushed as heads turned in our direction. Emotions tightened my throat as love for my family and my city overwhelmed me. These were the same people who had welcomed me, supported me and shown me nothing but love since I'd been crowned their queen. Now, I could share something close to my heart with them. Glancing at Kupua, he grinned and gave a nod of his head. "Go ahead, Ipo."

I lifted my voice to the crowd with tears brimming in my eyes and my voice wavering. "Today is a day of celebration! With the warmth of my love, it's my great joy to announce the birth of my niece, Okalani, newly born daughter of my sister, Rachel, and her husband, Mike. They are my family and yours, protectors and friends to our city. Like me, they were not born here, but have given you their hearts. I ask you to join me in welcoming Okalani to our family as an honorary citizen of Moku-ola. Join me in praying to the Creator for blessing and protection over her life. She will ever be in His care, as she is ours. Now, let us celebrate her birth!"

Roars erupted from the crowd as people whooped and cheered, jumping up and down and pumping fists. Drums pounded as dancing broke out and celebrations began throughout the city. Kupua and I walked over to a growing pile of gifts and messages for Okalani. Reaching down, I plucked one from the mass, turning it over in my hand. Written on a card attached were the words, *I will show you where to harvest the strongest kelp for rope making.* Inside the box lay a bracelet of rope, woven from the very kelp mentioned by the writer. Every gift held a promise to teach the child a skill to help her succeed in life. I smiled. Little Okalani would have so many watching out for her, ensuring her health and safety. Then I remembered someone who'd had those same benefits, but still suffered, and bit my lip, looking up at Kupua.

"Have you seen Eka? She wasn't at the pool."

He shook his head, frowning. "No, but she doesn't come out much these days, not since she started showing her pregnancy. She's probably at her mother's house, laying low."

"Yeah, but I thought she'd want to come see the baby. After all, her delivery is only a few weeks away and I know she was curious about how Rachel handled it." Eka had been reclusive since she'd announced she was carrying Moho's child and nobody had heard a word from him, which had me even more worried. Moho never seemed the type to give up and what he might be planning made me nervous. "Let's stop and check on her, okay?"

Kupua raised an eyebrow at me, "Okay, but what are you worried about?"

I shrugged. "Just want to make sure she's not depressed or losing hope. It can't be easy being pregnant with Moho's child. That baby is our family, too, which makes Eka our family, even if your brother rejects all of us."

"You're right. I guess I didn't think about it that way. Now I feel kinda bad I haven't gone to see her."

I twined my arm through his. "No worries. We'll take care of it right now."

We strolled down the path toward Eka's mother's house arm in arm, stopping to chat with friends along the way. So many eagerly wished us well and asked about the new baby. Eka's mom, Loli, lived at the south end of the city in a larger home built against a corner in the cavern wall. The family, known for making renowned waterproof clothing for Moku-ola, needed extra space for the sewing and manufacturing of their craft in large quantities. After her husband's death, Loli had enlisted his brother's sons to take on the family business and they'd moved in, relishing the opportunity to add their own designs to the family trade. Jake and Ezra also offered support to Eka, and I had hoped it would be enough to keep her spirits up.

Long, oblong pools lined the entryway to the front door, reaching deep into the sea, providing the family entry and exit points to the open ocean. These particular entry points led to areas where they harvested materials for the clothing we all loved. I dipped my hand in one, skimming warm water, relishing its feel against my skin. It'd been too long since my last swim. I'd have to get out soon, immerse myself in the ocean I loved.

Jake opened the front door before I had a chance to knock. His curly black hair bounced around his face, reminding me of Eka. He had curious eyes, constantly absorbing information around him, hungry for more, always learning. Those eyes bore into me as he swung the door open wide. "Queen Tessa, you've surprised us. Welcome to our home."

Stepping across the threshold I took his hand in mine. "Jake, we're hoping to talk to Eka, see how she's doing. Is she here?"

He glanced down at his feet, shuffling nervously. "She doesn't talk to anyone much anymore, even Ezra, who's always been her favorite." He motioned toward the back of the house, "she's in her room."

Loli stepped up behind Jake, fabric wrapped around one arm and the other glistening with moisture tinted purple. "Forgive me, Queen Tessa, for not greeting you at the door, but I've been working on some new designs."

I smiled at her, placing a hand on her shoulder. "Don't worry about it, Loli. We just stopped by to visit with Eka. Can we go back to her room?"

Her smile faded for a moment. "Of course, but she's not in a very good mood. It's been a tough few weeks for her and now with Rachel's delivery, she's even more upset. I'm so sorry she didn't come pay her respects, but I'm so glad you're here. Maybe you can talk some sense into her. She wants to find Moho and isn't listening to any of us. I don't know what to do."

Jake wrapped his arm around his aunt. "Yeah, but me and Ezra keep an eye on her. One of us is always close and won't let her leave." He met my eyes. "We love our cousin." His gaze flicked to Kupua. "No disrespect to you, but if I ever see Moho again I'm going to have to have a serious word with him about his attitude."

Kupua smiled and placed his hand on Jake's shoulder. "I'm right there with you Jake."

Jake nodded and ducked his head.

"Kupua and I will both do whatever we can to help. We all care about her." I led Kupua down the hall to Eka's room at the back of the house. Brightly colored fabrics lined both walls of the hall, rich patchworks of design and texture, leaving a faint smell of dye in the air. Eka's door stood out, plastered with her etchings. I shot Kupua a worried look. Each drawing depicted sharks, and in some Eka had included herself with a baby.

Shrugging, he knocked on the door. "Not surprising. She's carrying Moho's child, so of course she's thinking about him and wants to be close to him."

A sense of dread tugged my heart and I couldn't shake it, something seemed off. Behind the door, Eka's voice snapped. "Go away, I don't want to talk to anyone."

Pressing my head against the doorframe I replied, keeping my voice calm, "Eka, it's Tessa and Kupua. We just want to say hi. We won't stay long."

The door cracked and Ezra poked his head out, shorter than his brother, but same curly hair and piercing eyes. "Hey. Come on in." He swung open the door, revealing Eka, curled on her bed in the far corner with her back to us. Ezra quietly sat down in a well-worn chair wedged in the far corner under a lamp and set a book on his lap, leaving us on our own with Eka.

Kupua hung out by the door as I tip-toed to the bed, avoiding the numerous sketches scattered on the floor along with bits of charcoal and pencil shavings. Easing onto the edge of the bed, I whispered. "Eka, what's going on? Why are you avoiding everyone?"

She sniffed and stifled a sob. "I can't do this without him. I need to talk to Moho. If he knew about the baby, he'd care. I know it. He would want me with him."

"You might be right Eka, but it's not safe for you to travel, or risk the baby by going back to that volcano. You have to think of the baby."

She rolled over. Dark circles hung heavy under her eyes, which were reddened from crying. "I am. My child needs a father. You could send him a message and tell him I'm expecting. He has a right to know. Please, Tessa, at least try."

I sighed, choking back tears. Moho and Eka had a turbulent past and he was often cruel and emotionally abusive. What hope was there? "Even if I send out a message, I can't guarantee he'll respond, but I'll try if you'll start taking care of yourself. Get out of this room and spend time with friends. Deal?"

She sat up and flung her arms around me. Her wet cheeks dampened my neck as she clung to me. "Deal. Thanks so much, Tessa. This means the world to me."

I glanced over my shoulder at Kupua as dread crept down my spine and I considered Moho's possible response. Kupua shook his head, worry clouding his face, and stepped forward, reaching for my hand. Peeling myself from Eka's embrace, I grabbed hold of what he offered, knowing I couldn't do this alone. Together, we were stronger.

CHAPTER 3

MOHO

'AELIKE

DEAL

Revulsion roiled over me as I stepped onto dry land. Dirt and grime crunched beneath my feet. Trade winds whipped my hair from its tie and stung my cheeks, causing me to curse the need to travel above the surface. Just thinking about Henry sitting in a courtroom of surface dwellers stirred anger and bile in my gut. I needed him and today all delays would end and he would join me in the deep. Tessa may have gotten him arrested for his cache of illegal weapons, but his attorneys ensured his early release.

As agreed, he had a car waiting for me, along with a suit and shoes stiffer than oyster shells. The driver, a female with short, spikey blond hair smiled over her shoulder at me and winked.

I snorted as I slid into the back seat. "Not interested."

She huffed and accelerated onto the road and I hit the button to lift the glass partition separating us. Leaning back, I closed my eyes and reviewed our plan. Henry was out on bail after arraigned for weapons charges. My blood boiled just thinking about Tessa's interference. Luckily, my most powerful weapon had been tucked away somewhere else.

Henry's home on the big island hid my secret prize. Once we collected what we needed, Henry would join me at Seamount to set events in motion. Technically, Henry wasn't allowed to leave the state of Hawaii, but not many police could track beneath the sea.

Traffic thickened, stinking of exhaust and oil. When the limo finally stopped in front of Henry's estate, my nostrils burned from dry polluted air. How did people live like this? Shoving open the door, I knocked on the glass partition. "Stay here, be ready to leave."

Henry leaned against the door frame of his oversized mansion with arms crossed and expression hidden behind dark sunglasses. A smirk plastered his face, like a cat who'd swallowed a mouse. Impatience licked up my throat. "We need to make this quick, my sharks are waiting. This secret of yours better work as well as you claim."

He chuckled, straightening his tie and smoothing back his slick hair. "Of course, a deal's a deal. But remember, just because you possess something doesn't mean you know how to use it. It will take some training and practice."

I glowered and clenched my fists. Henry's smile faded and he gulped several times before speaking. "Luckily, you have me to show you. Partners, right?"

"Not partners. There is only one king and it is not you who sits on the throne. But, our agreement stands. Time's wasting. Where is it?"

He nodded. "Follow me."

Inside the gates of his estate, Henry led me through a cellar door hidden amongst the gardening shacks on his property. Stone steps descended deep into the earth, suffocating me with the musty stench of dirt, mold and rotting plants. Stagnant air clogged my throat. Reaching bottom, Henry unlocked an iron gate which creaked as its rusty hinges rebelled against being moved. We squeezed through into a small dank room no bigger than a large closet lined with shelves on one wall. Henry lifted a long wooden box off one of the shelves, laying it on the ground before me in a cloud of dust. Raising the top of the chest, he looked up from where he crouched on the ground and warned. "This has been in my family for centuries, handed down through generations, each being taught how to wield the weapon but cautioned against doing so because the consequences are too great. Even the small tsunami I created for you almost backfired. Do not take its power lightly."

"It gave us the diversion we needed. I am not afraid of power."

"You may not fear it, but you'd be wise to respect it. Once the weather is unleashed, it cannot be controlled."

Beneath the lid a spear glimmered, the handle embedded with diamonds and looking new as the day it'd been created. I leaned over and snatched it from its resting place. Much lighter than it appeared, the spear stretched above me several feet, colors shifting along the crystal shaft like clouds gliding across the sky. My voice whispered in awe. "The weather spear. It's beautiful." Leveling my gaze at Henry, I said, "you will teach me how to use it."

Henry stood and threw back his shoulders. "I will, but don't forget your promise to me. I'm not doing this for free. There is a wealth of sunken treasure in that ocean of yours just waiting for me to discover it. You will help me dig it up."

My grip on the spear tightened. "You will get your treasure."

He nodded. "Also, consider carefully before using this spear. What you unleash does not discriminate in its destruction. Weather is unpredictable, even if initiated by the spear, once in motion you won't be able to direct it. Your sharks could be at risk."

"I'll take my chances." Balancing the shaft in one hand, I strode from the cramped cellar into the blinding daylight and halted near his koi pond, which curved like a river around the border of his lawn. "Ready for instruction."

Sweat beaded on Henry's forehead as he licked his lips and positioned himself about a foot in front of me. "Always grip it with two hands before igniting its power so it stays steady. There's a bit of a kick, but mostly you want to control the aim."

Both my palms wrapped around the glistening handle and I nodded for him to continue.

"To create a wave like the tsunami, the spear must be in the water. Since we're not in the ocean, we'll direct it to the sky and whip up some wind. Rotate the spear to determine the severity, a full circle would create a tornado, a small flick is all we need to send the wind rushing across the island. Got it?"

"Yes, understood."

"Good. Let's start small. The large center diamond activates the spear. Press down with your thumb while stroking the stone on the opposite side."

I did as he said and the spear jolted to life, vibrating with enough power to knock me back a step.

"Told you it had some kick."

Blue and green light radiated from the shaft, sparking with electricity and throbbing in my hand. My hands clenched to keep it steady as it pulsed with energy.

"Now, raise it in the air and flick it slightly to the right. Careful not to move it too much, you don't want a tornado."

With a slight turn of my wrist, a gust of wind whirled and rushed ahead of me, sweeping leaves into its blustery vortex as it swooshed through trees and shrubs and blew across Henry's property and beyond. I lowered my arms and marveled at the instrument in my grasp. "Incredible."

Henry wiped sweat from his brow and exhaled. "In the ocean, you have to account for currents so it's harder to target a specific area. More of a rough guess really."

Excitement hummed through my veins as I considered the possibilities. "Besides waves, what else can it do undersea?"

"Impact jet streams, create whirlpools and underwater funnels, even set off deep sea volcanoes that have gone dormant. There may be more, but no one has ever tested its limits. At least not in my lifetime."

I nailed Henry with my stare. "Time to move this into the water."

CHAPTER 4

MOHO

'OLELO HO'OUNA 'IA

MESSAGE

As I approached my home a strange scent tinged the water around Seamount, burning my nostrils in warning. Sid, Tessa's octopus spy had been here, recently. Senses on high alert, Nikko, my best friend and shark, and I approached the entrance to Seamount, scanning the sea floor for more intruders. Seamount's volcano loomed above the surface, its shadow shifting shafts of light which filtered through the currents, playing tricks on my eyes. Below my feet, black tipped sharks patrolled, their hunger sparked by the scent of octopus nearby. Floating kelp tangled in my hair and I brushed it aside in frustration. Time to catch up with Henry, who traveled by submarine and would already be inside my home waiting, unless we'd been ambushed.

Nikko glided underneath the entrance. I propelled off his back and into the air lock tunnel, bursting through the surface, fists clenched for battle. A quick scan of the cavern revealed a plastic envelope wedged between rocks above the water line. I heaved myself onto dry land and snatched the note, ripping it open as water dripped on the page inside.

Moho, Eka requested I contact you to inform you of her situation. She loves you very much and is expecting a baby. You are going to be a father. She wants to see you but is not strong enough to travel. We offer a truce if you would like to arrange to visit her in Moku-ola. Queen Tessa

My throat tightened and I gasped for air, collapsing to my knees. Heat strangled my chest and my head spun with disbelief. A father? An unfamiliar spark of hope flickered from a dark recess of my heart. I was going to be a father. Warring emotions collided and a throbbing headache squeezed my head in a vice grip. Anger flared like a burning fire in my chest, revolting against the spark of joy ignited and reminding me of the plan Henry and I set in motion. My world tilted until a new perspective lodged in my brain. I had to get Eka out of Moku-ola and ensure the safety of my child. Nothing would stop me from protecting what belonged to me. Using the chunk of charcoal stuffed into the envelope I scribbled my response.

When night falls, I will wait at the family entrance to speak with Eka, but will go no further into the city. I will not honor the truce if Eka is harmed in any way.

I tore the paper and penned a separate note to send privately and eased back into the ocean, summoning two of my fastest Mako sharks. After delivering my commands I marched into the soul room to inform Henry of the change in plans. His eyes narrowed as he listened to my idea.

"You have to be joking, Moho. You're delaying our use of the spear to bring the little urchin here? We're supposed to be annihilating Moku-ola, not paying a social call."

My voice deepened to a growl. "I'm not asking your permission. Get your gear, we're leaving now so we can make it by nightfall. Remember who is King. You will follow my plan."

Darkness descended like a cloak over the ocean, and mammals sought refuge on land as predators emerged from the depths to hunt. Deep shadows moved with fluid grace, belying the deadly nature of their search.

Atop Nikko's back we sliced through the currents as one with Henry trailing in a submersible vehicle that looked like a yellow banana peel. One of the many toys he'd brought with him. Nearing the royal entrance to Moku-ola, he split off from Nikko and me. A white tipped oceanic shark guarded my flank as I swam through the crack in volcanic rock and broke the surface. My sharks thrashed and whipped the water into white froth in agitation until I laid a calming hand on their backs. "Easy, we won't be staying long."

Kupua, Kele, Tessa and Akalei gathered on the gravel beach, their movements echoing in the vast cavern. Soft, green light emanated from the rock walls, casting a sickly glow across their faces. Warm, sweet air caressed my cheeks as I inhaled the scent of my childhood home. A quick scan confirmed my suspicions. Eka was nowhere to be seen. I remained in the water between my restless guards.

"Where's Eka? Or was your truce a lie to lure me into this ambush?"

Tessa squatted near the edge, but not close enough to be yanked in, her arms crossed and chin lifted. "This is not an ambush. We can't allow the visit to occur this close to open-ocean where you could easily steal her away. She is safe and we plan to keep her that way. She doesn't even know about this meeting and won't unless you agree to meet inside the city. This is not negotiable."

My blood boiled. "You have no right to hold her hostage. It should be her choice, not yours. Entering the city is unacceptable and this only proves you cannot be trusted. Release Eka now!"

Tessa stood and slapped her hands against her thighs making a loud "ugh" sound. Kupua rubbed her shoulder and leveled his glare in my direction.

"Brother, we only wish to ensure the safety of the unborn child and have no desire to detain you or mislead you. Do you not care about this child? Do you not want to see Eka?"

Every muscle tensed as heat flushed my face. "Why is her safety at risk? Is she ill? How far along is she?"

Tessa shifted balance from foot to foot. "She's due in a few weeks."

Muscles in my neck and shoulders rippled with anger. "Why was I not told of the pregnancy sooner?"

"Moho, you haven't exactly been the attentive partner, or even interested in Eka's well-being. This is her home and we are doing our best to keep her safe. We didn't know if you'd even care about the baby."

"How I feel is none of your business. The child is not yours to protect and you have no right to interfere. All of you tread where you are not wanted. I am done. Make sure to inform Eka I came for her but you failed to allow the meeting." Submerging, I swung onto Nikko's back and we burst into open-ocean, the white tip trailing behind to ensure Kupua didn't attempt to follow. An unfamiliar panic clutched my chest. Worry. Henry had better have done his job.

CHAPTER 5

TESSA

NALOWALE

GONE

"Don't worry Tessa, you did the right thing. We couldn't take a risk with Eka and the baby. Moho is unpredictable and who knows how he might have reacted if she'd been here." Kupua tugged me into a hug but it didn't help. Sorrow and regret choked me. We'd failed to bring Moho to Eka and I knew she desperately wanted to speak to him.

I pushed away and clasped his hand, waving for Akalei and Kele to join us. "Let's check on Eka and let her know what happened. We should have told her what we were doing." My chest tightened, guilt burning like a stingray's barb.

Akalei nudged my arm and frowned. "Something isn't right about all this. Moho doesn't usually give up so easily."

"It did seem like he was a little too eager to leave after bothering to come at all." I examined her face and bit my lip. "What do you think he's up to?"

Kupua pulled me farther down the hall. "With Moho, you can never be sure. I'll feel better once we make sure Eka's safe at home."

When we arrived at Eka's home her front door hung slightly ajar. I peeked inside and called out, "Hello. Anyone home?"

Silence. I glanced over my shoulder. "You all wait here. I'm going to do a quick search of her room and be right back."

"Dis no good. Nuttin but bad happen round Moho."

Placing my finger over my mouth, I shot Kele a glare before pivoting to jog down the hallway. Eka's room was in the back of the house. Even from the hall I could hear the trickle of water off a fountain in the corner, but no human movement. Charcoal drawings covered the floor of her bedroom like forgotten treasures. A rocking chair in the corner creaked softly as if it had only recently been vacated, but no Eka. I rushed back to my friends. "She's not here."

Akalei moaned. "She hasn't left her room for weeks. Where could she have gone?"

"Queen Tessa." Eka's mother shouted from the side of the house, near their ocean tide pool. She burst around the corner, panting, eyes red and swollen. "Queen Tessa. Eka's gone. She's left us." Trembling, she shoved a note into my hand. I steadied her by wrapping an arm around her shoulder.

Mom, I'm so sorry I couldn't say good-bye but please don't worry about me. I'm with Moho and he wants to take care of the baby and me. We belong with him. We are safe. Eka

Sadness choked me. "She left to be with Moho. We should have known he was up to something."

"Please, Queen Tessa, you have to go after her. She can't deliver the baby all alone. You have to bring her back." Desperation laced her words as she pleaded, cutting through my heart like a knife.

"We'll do what we can but we can't force her to return against her will. She's old enough to choose who she wants to live with. I'm so sorry."

Tears slid down her cheeks as she snatched the note from my hand and stumbled into her home, mumbling under her breath. "My baby."

Kupua sidled next to me. "Moho likely has her at Seamount by now."

I glanced at him, dread forming a knot in the pit of my stomach. "You're probably right, but we should do a patrol of the area just in case. I don't want to take any chances he's hanging around to cause more trouble. He didn't pull this off by himself. Even Moho can't be in two places at once."

"I go dis way and see if I can catch up to Moho," Kele called over his shoulder before diving into the pool next to Eka's house that lead into open water.

Akalei sighed. "Always the hero. His heart is so big it sometimes blocks out his brains."

Kupua shrugged. "We better follow him. If he does catch up to Moho, he'll need our help."

CHAPTER 6

TESSA

MAKANI PAHILI

HURRICANE

Schools of Bluestripe Butterfly fish swarmed us, darting between our legs and coral in the reef as they searched for meals. Trade winds shifted southward for the winter, picking up speed and cooling the surface. Lizzy zipped across my path, twirling and diving as she searched the waters with her super sea lion speed. Sid tightened his grip on my ankle, his tentacles tickling as they squeezed. The bands on my wrists glowed bright green, shooting light to guide my path. The bands also allowed me to breathe underwater, a gift from the Creator. Since I was not born in Moku-ola, I could not breathe underwater without the bands like my friends. We caught up to Kele, who hovered in the water with one hand resting on Ka, Kupua's faithful turtle. He frowned and shook his head. No sign of Moho or Eka anywhere. Silt clouded the surrounding sea and currents increased in intensity. The oceans mood was shifting.

Kicking to the surface I bobbed my head above water. Wind whipped and forced me to squint against the torrents of rain pounding the waves as they churned. Swells crested at six feet and the four of us had to dive under each one to avoid being crushed. Kupua, shouted above the thunder of angry ocean. "These waves are pretty intense. I don't like the look of this. Could be a hurricane's coming. A real nasty one."

"Head home," I shouted, and dove as another wave crashed over my head. A bright light flashed and a sea lion splashed in Kupua's place. Furry mouths latched onto my arms as Lizzy and Kupua hauled me deeper, faster until we were back inside the family entrance. My knees scraped on the rough gravel as I crawled from the water and took several deep breaths to calm my racing pulse. "Do you think it's going to get worse out there?"

Kele plopped his thick body down next to me, while Akalei scooted close on my other side and wrapped her slender arm around my shoulders. Kupua leaned against the rock wall, back in human form and shaking droplets from his shaggy hair. "Most certainly. The storm's just beginning."

"Guess we're done with patrol for awhile." Rubbing Lizzy under the chin, I instructed her, "Tell our scouts to come back here to wait out the storm. We don't want anyone getting injured in this weather. And, hurry, don't take any chances with your own safety."

She barked and I kissed her nose before she lumbered into the water, her flippers spraying small rocks in her wake. I scrambled to my feet, brushing gravel from my legs. Kupua clasped my hand and I leaned my head against his shoulder as we strolled through the tunnel. "How long do these hurricanes usually last?

"It should blow through in the next twenty-four hours, nothing to worry too much about."

Someone's stomach rumbled and Akalei giggled. "Hey, Tessa, Kele's hungry.

"What else is new?" I flashed him a smile over my shoulder. "You're as bad as Puna."

"Fo' real? He try to keep wit me but I one tough braddah wit the ginds. I da food king."

Puna was Mike's older and much bigger brother who prided himself on traditional Hawaiian cooking. "I'll tell him you said that next time we're on Lanai and we'll see what he thinks."

Kele grunted. "No worries. Bring on da challenge."

Kupua and I laughed as we placed our hands on the carved door to our home and the locks clicked, cracking open and spilling soft light into the tunnel. "You all go ahead and eat, I'm going to spend some time with Rachel and my adorable niece."

Kupua kissed the top of my head. "Come eat when you're done, Ipo."

My face flushed and I stretched on my tip-toes to hug him. "Will do."

Rachel, Mike and the baby had settled into the room next to mine until Kele medically cleared the baby to return to their home on Lanai. Secretly, I suspected he was delaying to give me more time with my new niece. I knocked quietly hoping not to wake the baby. Mike cracked the door. "Hey, come on in. Rachel's been hoping you'd visit soon."

Rachel lay propped on a dozen pillows in her bed with the baby ensconced in a basket, sleeping next to her. Sheer white fabric billowed from each of the four posts of her bed giving the effect of floating clouds around her small form. Her face glowed as she beamed and motioned for me to join her under the blankets. I snuggled next to the basket and peeked at my niece whose tiny mouth moved in sucking motions as she dreamed of her momma. The air around her smelled of baby powder and milk, sparking an ache in my heart. "She's so beautiful."

Rachel tucked a blanket around her tiny daughter. "Yeah, pretty amazing."

"Do you feel different being a mom?"

She nodded and bit her lip. "It's like my whole world has shifted. Things I used to care about seem silly. All that matters is keeping her safe and happy." She held my gaze with tears brimming in her eyes. "Family, loved ones, our life together, that's all that really matters. I'm so grateful for all of you. I love you, sis."

I wrapped my arms around her and buried my face in her shoulder. "Love you, too." My sister was my only family and had always been my rock. She was the stabilizing force in my life. I may have to keep Moku-ola a secret from the world, but I had made it clear that she and Mike would be part of my life as queen.

"Not long now and we'll be celebrating your wedding day. Are you ready?"

I straightened the sheets, tucking them around me. "I think so. I love Kupua and have never been more sure of how I feel. I'm just not sure I'll know how to be a wife. I don't want to disappoint him."

She curled her hand around mine and the warmth of her touch calmed my nerves. She'd always been that for me, the calm in my storm. "You are a great queen and you'll be a great wife as well. Listen to him and love him and it will work out. He's a good man. And that's saying a lot coming from your big sister. I'm not easy to please."

My cheeks flushed with heat. "How did you feel when you married Mike? Were you scared?"

"It wasn't so different. I may not have been queen but I was carrying more responsibility than most women my age. It seemed overwhelming at the time and yet, now seems like no big deal."

A lump formed in my throat. Rachel had raised me after our parents died and Mike had taken me in as his own. Without them, who knows what would have happened to me. My forehead leaned against hers. "You'll always be my home."

"And now we've added two more, little Okalani and your Kupua."

Mike cleared his throat. "What happened with Moho? Is he in the city visiting Eka? Makes me nervous having him around."

I released Rachel's hand and frowned at Mike. "No, he never entered the city, but Eka's vanished. She snuck out to be with him. We did a sweep of the surrounding ocean and everything looked clear. No sign of anything except the hurricane."

Mike's eyes widened. "Hurricane? When did that happen? Why didn't you say something? Puna's up there and so is Hiiaka. How bad is it? Do we need to warn them?"

"Kupua says it's nothing to worry about. He didn't seem concerned. If he thought his mother was in any danger, he would have done something."

Mike ran his hands through his thick black hair and paced the room. "I don't know Kika, hurricanes aren't always predictable." He glanced at Rachel. "Glad you two are down here though, safest place to be in a hurricane."

I leaned into a soft down pillow and yawned. "I'm sure it'll be okay."

I must have dozed off because I opened my eyes to discover Rachel asleep next to me and Mike snoring in a rocking chair in the corner. His rough, grumbling, roar permeated the room with a strange masculine comfort. My stomach rumbled. How long had I been asleep? I slowly eased off the bed, careful not to jostle the basket and crept out the room to track down some food.

Kupua perched on the edge of the room overlooking the city, his expression somber. Below, the sacred pool shimmered in the soft light glimmering through the volcanic walls and the only movement came from a lone sea lion fumbling to find a comfortable position among his pile of family members. I settled next to Kupua, carefully juggling my plate of sliced pineapple. "It's so peaceful when the city's this quiet."

He nodded. "Sid reports the storm's getting worse outside our walls. Waves are cresting at over sixty feet. Underwater the turbulence is intense and oxygen levels are dropping to dangerous levels. Even though the shallow temperatures are cooling, which should calm the hurricane, it only seems to be intensifying."

My stomach churned. "What does all that mean?"

"It means this storm isn't acting consistent with the laws of nature. It's odd, almost like it has a mind of its own with evil intent." He twisted his head to look me in the eye. "Want to venture a guess as to why?"

I shivered. "It's not possible. He can't control the weather. Can he?"

"He shouldn't be able to summon a megaladon, but we both know he did."

CHAPTER 7

MOHO

KULEANA

RESPONSIBILITY

"Moho," Eka exclaimed as I swept her into my arms and clasped her newly round form tight to my chest. She sobbed against my shoulder and for once I allowed it, turmoil roiling in my stomach. Newly sprouted emotions spread their tendrils through my heart. The need to protect her, care for her, blossomed in my chest and its warmth melted what once had been cold and dead. Between gasps she choked out words. "I…didn't know if…you'd want the baby…I missed you so much."

Henry had kept his word and brought her safely to Seamount in his submarine. She was in my home, tucked into the underwater caverns beneath the volcano, which loomed above my domain. I held her at arms-length to better see her face. "You carry my son or daughter, a royal child. You and the baby are my responsibility and your place is here, in my kingdom. I will take care of both of you. We will not be separated again." As soon as the words escaped my lips, my heart swelled in agreement, but, at the same time, confusion clouded my mind. A voice raked through my ears. *You are mine. Your loyalty is pledged to me. Do not forget your promise to deliver royal blood. This girl is a distraction. Give her to me.* The Lua Pele reached into my soul like a poison, spreading death through my veins. Though it lived in dark tunnels and secretive lairs throughout the ocean depths, the Lua Pele's existence was more than physical, its dark presence transcended into the spiritual realm. Nobody had seen the creature and survived to talk about it. Not even me.

Releasing Eka, I collapsed to one knee as hot pokers exploded through my skull with the Lua Pele's words. Sharp jabs of pain sliced down my chest but something else ignited as well. The newly found warmth in my heart offered some measure of comfort against the onslaught of agony. An instinct to protect battled with the Lua Pele's demand for obedience. My voice rasped in a hoarse whisper. "I will keep my promise, but you cannot have my child. That was not part of our agreement."

You promised me royal blood. I tire of waiting.

"Soon. I have a plan," I moaned and grit my teeth to keep from releasing a cry of anguish. Pain twisted and rolled inside me like I'd swallowed a bucket of hot nails.

Your time is running out. Do not fail me.

Slowly the pain receded and I inhaled a deep breath. Fear shone in Eka's eyes as they spilled with tears. Her delicate hand rested on my shoulder, soft and warm.

"What just happened? Who were you talking to Moho?"

Pushing from the ground, I stood and faced her. "Do not worry, everything is fine."

Hurt flit across her expression before she glanced away.

Henry sneered from the corner. "Not good timing, Moho. Eka's going to mess up everything we've been working for. Your emotions are blinding you."

I glared at him "This is not your business. Our plans do not change and you are not to speak to Eka. Leave us."

He returned my stare for a few moments before huffing and stomping from the room. My attention returned to Eka, who trembled before me, her face streaked with tears. "Let's get you settled. You're not to travel in the ocean anymore, until after the baby's born. I'll escort you to our room and then I've got work to do."

The tight curls of her hair bounced as she swung her head from side to side. "I don't want to be alone. Please don't leave."

I gripped her arm and nudged her down the tunnel to our rooms. "Eka, there's work I must finish. It's for our future. I've stocked the room with drawing supplies so you won't be bored and I promise to return as soon as I can."

An hour later I tore myself from Eka and stalked to the ocean with the weather spear clasped in my fist. Henry waited, leaning against the rock wall with a smirk plastered on his face. "Our plan's working."

"You mean my plan. I knew Tessa's little friends couldn't handle the hurricane and would start vacating the area or die. We just need to wait. She and Kupua will eventually investigate. They're so predictable."

"Your sharks aren't hanging around too close, either. Is that part of your plan?"

Hot rage rumbled in my gut as I considered knocking the smirk from his face. A tick pulsed in his jaw, a sure sign the pause in my steps made him nervous. "They're safe, just where I want them."

His gaze flicked to the spear. "If you keep whipping up the storm it might backfire on you. Why risk it when the storm's already raging just fine?"

"Didn't anyone ever tell you more is better? Besides, the situation's changed and I'd like to move things along faster than we originally planned." Power pulsed through the spears' shaft and into my hand. It called to me, inviting me to bask in its potency like a drug.

A line formed between his brows and his eyes hardened. "You mean Eka. I'm warning you, Moho, don't let that irritating urchin cloud your judgment. She's trouble. You can't afford to get soft now."

My fingers twitched and tightened on the spear. I shoved past him and leapt into the water where Nikko thrashed impatiently. Henry could not follow me into the ocean, at least not without his submarine. Being born on the surface, he lacked the ability to breathe underwater, unless he was in direct contact with a citizen of Moku-ola.

Nikko's rough skin scraped against mine as we rocketed to the surface. Turbulent currents yanked at us, but Nikko's powerful body cut through the churn like a knife through soft butter. Waves swelled at the surface, pounding us as I lifted the spear into the air and activated its power. Its energy connected to a darkness in my heart, animating me with a sense of strength and the cold certainty that nothing could defeat me. The ocean roared in response. Winds immediately intensified and howled their fury across the sea. Salty licks of water slashed and stung my face. Funnels of water reached into the sky and swirled in chaotic frenzy on every side of us like tornados on steroids. The chill in my heart fed on the maelstrom, craving more, demanding more. Desire for power clamored until it drowned out all other thoughts and reeked havoc on my mind. The spear held sway over my very soul.

Amid the tumult, a whisper of a voice cracked through the chaos. *You have a choice. Fight back my son.* The recent warmth born in my heart reached for the Creator, recognizing truth in his words. I focused on that spark, latching on to the only hope left to me of wrenching free of the spear. My fingers relinquished their grip on the shafts ignition jewel and suddenly my arm felt as if it carried the weight of a ton of bricks and slammed into the sea. A shudder convulsed through my body. Shaken, I kicked Nikko's side, my hand still clutching the spear.

Nikko and I dove deep. Despite the loss of control, a sense of accomplishment burst in my chest and the familiar icy grip on my heart restored its hold. It wouldn't be long now. Very soon I'd have the royal blood I needed to appease the Lua Pele and my vow would be fulfilled.

CHAPTER 8

TESSA

MAKAUKAU

PREPARATION

Akalei rested her chin on my shoulder. Her minty breath tickled my ear. "It's perfect. You look beautiful."

I ran my hands down the lace hugging my waist. "You sure it isn't too much?"

"No. It's exactly right for a queen."

I gazed at the mirror in wonder at my own reflection. Poised like a doll, I stood draped in a green wedding dress, the sweetheart neckline and bodice layered in lace, which flared to ankle length toule dotted with flecks of mother of pearl. A sash of chiffon, braided with beads made from the same mother of pearl, wrapped my waist. Although my feet remained bare, Akalei had sprinkled glitter, shaved from pearls, across my toes so they sparkled.

Eka's mom checked the length. "I think we're done. No more fittings for you, this dress is ready for the big day."

I glanced over my shoulder at Akalei. "What are we going to do with my hair?"

She ran her fingers through my long auburn locks. "You'll wear your crown. I'll think of some ideas. We have a couple weeks."

Rachel burst into the room and halted when she caught my reflection, her eyes wide and fingers covering her mouth. She slowly lowered her hand. "You look amazing."

I swiveled and hugged her tight. She smelled of fresh baby powder and innocence. "Thanks, Sis."

Her arms wrapped me in their warmth, clasping me against her, where for a moment, I was a little sister once again. "I'm sorry to interrupt your fitting, but Kupua asked me to come get you. Something is wrong, and he wouldn't tell me what. Did you know he could be so stubborn? Not an attractive trait in a brother-in-law. Anyway, he needs you right away."

I untied the sash at my waist. "Okay, just give me a minute to change."

Moments later, Akalei, Rachel and I all hustled through the house to the room overlooking our city where Kupua and Kele waited. I rushed to Kupua's side and grabbed his hand, glimpsing the worry shifting in his eyes. "What's happened?"

"The storm's worsened. It's more powerful than any we've experienced before. So many sea turtles have died it may take decades to recover."

My gut wrenched. "Is Ka safe?"

"Yes, she's here with some of her family, but others haven't been so lucky. Coral reefs around the islands are breaking apart and thousands of fish have perished. We may be safe here, but I fear for our loved ones on the surface and can't sit here and do nothing."

"What can we do?"

"I'm going for my mother and your uncle. Kele and I can swim deep beneath the turbulence until we reach Lanai. We'll bring them both to the city where they'll be safe. It's too dangerous to leave them on the surface." Hiiaka had chosen to leave Moku-ola to live on land after crowning me queen. She'd wanted to give me time to find my rhythm in leadership without relying too much on her. We all missed her. My uncle had never seen Moku-ola and was one of the few surface dwellers that knew of its existence.

"What then? If Moho's causing this storm, we've gotta go after him and try to stop it. We can't allow this destruction to continue."

Kele shook his head and stepped closer to Kupua. "Nevah. Dat idea is crazy. Moho lookin fo' beef wit you and it no good on his turf." Kele paced, raking his short hair with both hands.

"I get it Kele. Moho wants us to come to him, but there might be a way to turn the tables."

Akalei grinned. "You have an idea."

"I do. But first, I agree with Kupua that we need to get Hiiaka and Puna safe."

Kupua raised his eyebrow. "I never said you were coming. I'd argue you don't need to help but something tells me it won't change your mind."

I patted his shoulder. "Good call. Let's get this done."

He rolled his eyes, grabbed my hand and led the way out to the ocean.

We hugged the sea floor to avoid the storm's turbulent churn closer to the surface. As we neared Lanai and shallower water, chunks of coral swirled in the currents, broken from nearby reefs. Bodies of dead fish tumbled with the surf, which rose at least twenty to thirty feet before crashing against the shore. Silt clouded the water and impaired our vision, leaving a gritty taste in my mouth. We rode a wave onto land, and struggled for footing. Kupua shouted, "We're lucky, we're in the eye of the storm but don't have much time. Hurry." Palm trees hung bent and snapped under the force of howling gusts. If we didn't get back underwater before the eye passed, we may not be able to get back at all. My feet dug into the beach. Rain drenched my back, causing my sandy clothing to cling against my skin. It felt a little like being ground with sand paper.

We reached the asphalt parking lot and linked hands, our backs to the push of wind. Kupua yanked me to a stop and I heard my name being shouted above the roar. Clinging to a cement post not far from where we stood was Hiiaka. I pointed and propelled us in her direction. She clutched my outstretched hand and collapsed into Kupua's arms. Tremors shook her arms and exhaustion deepened the lines around her eyes.

Each of us kept one arm tight around her waist as we rotated back towards the crashing waves. Torrents of rain at our backs thrust us to the edge of the water where Kupua dove and bright light flashed. A black and white form broke the surface in his place, a massive orca. Smashing my nose up against Hiiaka's, I shouted, "Do you have enough strength left to hold onto Kupua's back?"

Resolve hardened her eyes and she nodded. Together we splashed against the surf, submerging beneath the crashing waves and latching onto Kupua. He torpedoed into the depths until we outpaced the storms reach. Relief loosened the muscles I didn't even realize I'd been clenching. Kupua quickly emerged into our homes entrance where Kele dragged Hiiaka onto the gravel. Her chest heaved and her limbs trembled. She closed her eyes a moment before speaking.

"Thank you for coming for me. I was on my way here and thought I could make it to the sea on my own but the winds were too much for me."

"What about Puna? Do you know where he is? We have to return for him."

She waved her hand. "No. He and his family evacuated to a shelter on O'hau. They are all safe. Nobody's left on Lanai."

Kupua joined us, shaking water from his hair. "Why didn't you go with them, Mother?"

"I knew something was wrong with this storm and wanted to help. I was on my way to the city when the storm intensified and you all showed up." She sat up straight and leveled her gaze at Kupua. "This is Moho's doing, isn't it? He's behind the hurricane?"

"We think so." He motioned in my direction. "Tessa has a plan."

CHAPTER 9

TESSA

MAUNU

BAIT

Kupua and I hitched a ride on currents far enough below the storm to avoid the worst of the turbulence. Astride his back and gripping his dorsal fin, I shuddered. Traveling on a fifteen-foot tiger shark, even though I knew it was Kupua, set my nerves on edge. Darkness pressed against the edges of light cast by my wristbands in the murky water. Somewhere between Moku-ola and Seamount, we patrolled and waited for Moho to take our bait.

A sunken ship loomed in the shadows beneath us, its hull protruding from silt as if planted for décor in a fish tank. Small blue sharks skirted its edges, fleeing into holes as Kupua drew closer. I swiped my hand across Kupua's rough skin, craving contact and reassurance. Red marks scratched my palms where we made contact. My nerves tingled as I sensed Moho and his shark approach. Kupua ducked into a ravaged cabin on the ship and a shiver ran through me in anticipation. We wanted to lure Moho away from Seamount, not actually have a confrontation with him.

A flash of gray whooshed past the hole we peeked from, Moho's leg gripping its side. We waited, hidden within the vacuum of the wreckage.

When Moho and Nikko didn't swing past a second time, I urged Kupua forward, anxious to return home and learn if our plan had worked. We glided along the bulkhead of the ship, avoiding open sea until we were sure he'd moved on.

With a flick of his caudal fin, Kupua jetted toward home. As soon as we left the safety of the ship a surge of current knocked us into a spin. My grip on Kupua loosened and I tumbled off his back as he attempted to gain control. I kicked my legs and arms and flailed against the powerful current, but my body continued to roll in its grip. Suddenly, the water stilled as if on command. Dread pressed upon my heart as I scanned the area with light from my wristbands, searching for Kupua. My beam sliced through darkness and illuminated a dozen oceanic white tipped sharks surrounding me. With a gasp, I immediately dove deeper, calling for Kupua through the connection we shared with our minds. He responded, rising from the depths he'd been spun into.

Before he came into view, a white tip bumped my side with its nose, then swerved away in a wide arc around my position. Another blocked my descent by flashing inches in front of my outstretched hands. I backpedaled, gulping fear as they closed in. Their long, flat bodies created a wall of gray between me and freedom. Kupua emerged from below, rocketing through the circle of sharks and I clutched at his pectoral fin as he zoomed past. Before he could sweep us beyond the shiver of sharks, a white tip clamped onto my leg sending piercing pain shooting through my body. I cried out but held tight to Kupua, despite the wrenching weight of the shark shaking my leg like I was caught in a wood chipper. My head spun and just as I thought I could no longer hold on the shark released me. Pain arched through my muscles. Sensing my panic, Kupua sped us toward home.

White tips could not match the speed of a tiger and soon we were far from their reach. I wrapped both arms around Kupua's fin hugging him against my chest and fought the dark fog of unconsciousness pressing against my thoughts. My leg dangled, blood trailing a ribbon of red in our wake.

The moment we entered the waters of Moku-ola, Kupua transformed and surfaced with his arms around me. My head fell against his shoulder and blackness overtook me.

I woke to the smell of garlic, lavender and rosemary. Blinking, I scanned the room. Long, green, bandages hung from the ceiling and voices murmured close by. It appeared I was in Kele's medical clinic in Moku-ola. My leg throbbed with a dull ache and when I attempted to scoot upright the room spun like a top.

Kele rushed to my side. "Nuff already, my queen. Don't tink you can get up cuz you need rest. Stay in bed."

I smiled weakly at him. "No worries. I'll follow doctors orders."

"Fo'real?"

"Yeah. For real. Where's Kupua?"

Akalei approached the other side of the bed and laid her hand on my arm. "He'll be here in a minute. He went to get some food from the kitchen for you. We've been worried, Tessa." She gripped me and helped me sit upright, stuffing pillows behind my back for support.

"Thanks." I squeezed her hand. "What happened at Seamount? Did you find Eka?"

Her face dropped. "Yes. Eka was at Seamount and we talked to her, but she refused to leave. She's convinced Moho loves her and will take care of her and the baby. We tried, Tessa. Eka's made her choice and will not budge."

"At least we know she's alive and safe for now. Her mom isn't going to be happy." I turned to Kele. "What about when she delivers? Will Moho know what to do?"

Kele shook his head. "No. Da brah has no medical skills. He da fighter not da healer."

Akalei bit her lip. "She told us something else. According to Eka, Moho has some sort of spear he claims can control the weather. She wanted to warn us to be careful."

Kupua strolled into the healing room carrying a platter of steaming noodle soup and crackers. My mouth watered. He set the tray on my lap and rested his cheek against the top of my head, wrapping his arms around my body. "You scared me out there. How're you feeling?"

I inhaled the sweet smell of ocean clinging to him and fought back the lump in my throat. "Not my best day, but I'll be okay."

Kele shook his finger at me. "Try stay off your feet. Kay den?"

"I promise to follow instructions, Kele." Scooping soup, I sucked it off the spoon, relishing the warm broth as it slid down my throat. My stomach growled. I hadn't realized how hungry I was. Between gulps of noodles, I fired a question to my doctor. "How long do I have to stay in bed?"

Kupua spoke before Kele could answer. "We want to put you in the healing pool to speed up the process so you won't be in bed more than a few days. You up for that?"

I set aside the tray and peeled back my covers. "I'm for anything that'll get me out of this bed."

Kupua swept me into his arms. A sharp dagger of pain exploded in my leg and then slowly settled into a throbbing ache. "How bad is it?"

He whispered against my hair. "Bad enough. You're going to have a pretty nasty scar and are lucky to still have a leg."

I sucked in breath. "It happened so fast. Did you see Moho?"

"No. But I'm sure he was watching. That surge came out of nowhere. It wasn't natural. We've been talking and think he's found a way to control the weather."

I leaned my head against his chest. "Akalei just told me about the spear. How do we fight something like that? How can we stop this hurricane?"

He carried me a few steps and eased me into the steaming pool. "Right now just focus on healing and regaining your strength."

Deep volcanic lava naturally heated the water in the pool, which streamed from a source deep in the underground rock. Kele added healing herbs to create the steaming blend of garlic, lavender and rosemary.

Hot water soaked into my muscles as they relaxed and I submerged to my chin. Tension and pain evaporated through my pores like steam from a kettle. The dull throbbing in my leg lessened. Inhaling deep breaths, I blissed out.

Kupua sat cross-legged on the ledge above the waterline and watched me, his eyebrows scrunched together in a frown. I knew that look. He was in deep thought. I decided not to poke the bear and closed my eyes, relishing the soothing soak.

Akalei tapped my shoulder and I jerked from drowsing off. "Sorry, Tessa. Kele says it's time to wrap your leg."

"How long have I been in here?" I lifted my hands from the water to find they had wrinkled like raisins. "Did I fall asleep?"

"Yeah. You've been soaking for over an hour."

I sighed. "This pool is awesome. Can't I sleep in here?"

Kupua chuckled and reached to lift me from the water. "Kele jokes that it's better than any spas on the surface and he should know." He heaved me dripping from the pool and carried me to the table Kele had prepared to change my bandages. As soon as it hit air my leg throbbed again.

Kupua handed me a towel and stacked pillows behind my back so I could watch Kele's work in comfort. Kele gently peeled off layers of wet seaweed gauze, dropping them into a bucket at his feet with a plop. He made them himself with a special mix of healing herbs. Cool air chilled my leg as he removed the last layer and revealed a ragged tear along my calf, neatly stitched together but still red and puffy. Kupua tensed next to me and I grabbed his hand. Through our connection his anger surged like an explosion of red hot lava. His voice rumbled. "He will not put you in danger again."

I laid my head against his arm and stroked my hand along his caramel skin, calming the storm that raged in his heart. "It doesn't look too bad. Nice work, Kele."

Kele winked at me and kept working, his fingers applying a thick green paste over the wound. "Dis will numb it and keep out infection."

The throbbing stopped almost immediately and I released a breath as pain receded. Once the wound was covered in paste, he wrapped green gauze bandages around my leg until no skin was visible from my knee down. He tied off the last piece and pinned me with his sternest glare. "You stay la'dat. No move fo' today." His gaze shifted to Kupua. "You two talk story. I going to get some rest. Make sure your wahine gets da rest to." He snatched the bucket and trudged out of the room with Akalei trailing. She flashed me a smile over her shoulder and waved.

Kupua covered me with a blanket and sunk into a chair. Lines carved his face from worry and exhaustion. "Is there any chance you want to sleep and talk about this weather spear later?"

"Not likely."

CHAPTER 10

TESSA

PAHELE

TRAP

A week later I paced the length of the sacred pool, biting my lip and tapping my fingers against my hips. My limp was almost gone and only a distant pain nagged at me if I walked too long without resting. Kele was a miracle worker. "The winds may have died down but Sid reports a whirlpool funnel about 2 miles North of the islands, in the middle of the Pacific. We all know that's not normal. It's throwing off ocean currents and messing with whale migrations."

Kupua held out his arm to stop me in my tracks. "It's not your fault."

With a quick sidestep, I avoided his attempt to block me and kept pacing. "I know, but we have to get hold of this spear of Moho's. Eka may not want to leave but we're going to have to return and steal it."

"Agreed. Sneaking in is easy for me. I can disguise my appearance. I think I should go alone….and before you argue, hear me out."

I huffed and frowned at him. "Go on."

"You know the more of us breaking in, the easier it will be for him to detect the breach. We have a much better chance at success if one of us goes alone and I'm the best choice. If I go in as something small, like a tiny sand crab, he won't even know I'm there." His gaze landed on me. "Can you say the same?"

I tipped my head back and sighed, knowing he was right, but not liking it one bit. "Fine. But Kele and I will be close, just in case something goes wrong. And you have to promise to give me a play by play with your thoughts while you're inside."

He grabbed my hand and tugged me into his arms. "Agreed."

I kissed his neck and inhaled his sweet scent, fighting the worry creeping into my heart. Nothing ever went as planned when it came to Moho.

Into his hair I whispered. "A crab is the smallest creature you've changed into since I've known you. How is it possible for you to become so tiny?"

He chuckled in my ear, tickling my neck with his warm breath. "It's second nature to me now, but at first it took some practice. When the creature I change into is too small for me to absorb into, some of my body mass is thrown into clear particles surrounding the animal. Not detectible by most eyes."

"Does it hurt?"

"No. It's a gift from the Creator and brings me joy, not pain. Because of this gift, I have greater insight into the lives we protect in the sea. Knowing his creation with a depth I could not have achieved without this gift. A true miracle."

My finger traced along his jaw. "Everything about you is a miracle."

He caught my finger between his lips and my stomach flipped. He moved his kiss from my finger to my hand. "You are the best gift the Creator ever gave me. My heart is yours, Ipo."

"And mine is yours, Kupua."

The next morning, we swam toward Seamount accompanied by a pod of dolphins who insisted on providing back up. Fin and his family glided through the rough sea, keeping us at the center of the pod. Kupua swam in dolphin form and I straddled his back, holding tight to his dorsal fin. Seaweed gauze was double wrapped around my wound, even though it was almost fully healed. Kele's idea.

The farther we traveled, the more the ocean calmed, turbulence easing until we broke free from the storm's reach. Above the waves, raging wind died to a slight breeze, tickling the gentle swells. As we neared Seamount, the pod swerved to a nearby circular oceanic coral reef where we'd wait on Kupua. I slid from his back and pressed my cheek against his slick skin. "Please be careful."

His love washed over me before he transformed into a tiny crab and propelled toward the Seamount entrance. His tiny pinchers snapped as he flitted through the sea. *Our plan will work.* He sent through his thoughts. I settled onto the sandy bottom and prayed he would be safe.

I'm inside. Kupua sent his thoughts. *It's quiet. I'm going to explore and try to locate the spear.*

Fin nudged me with his nose and I kissed the top of his head. "Thanks, my friend. All is well so far. Better do a sweep to check for sharks. Nikko is bound to be patrolling somewhere in the area."

He flicked his tail and jetted out of view. A triggerfish nipped my fingers, reminding me this was his territory and wondered how long I might be staying. His oversized head, green body and florescent orange stripes made him one of the most unique species in the area. I rubbed his head with my index finger and reassured him I would not be a permanent competitor for his space. He grumbled and examined me for algae, tickling the skin along my arm and bringing a smile to my face.

Kupua checked in. *Still no sign of Moho. I'm in the soul room, near his throne and the spear is leaning against it. I've got to change forms to carry it. I'll be right out.*

After alerting Fin, I shifted positions and moved to my knees, ready to flee quickly if needed. My nerves tingled as I waited, adrenaline pulsing through my veins.

I've got it! On my way…wait. Something's wrong. No….Tessa get out of here. Now.

Fin buzzed my head, spinning and crying an alarm with Nikko in pursuit. Two dolphins from his pod swept beside me and I clutched at one of their fins and they rocketed from the area. Kupua would not or could not respond to my call so I reached out for Kele, initiating plan B. I ordered my dolphin escort to halt and we hovered in the water while my brain scrambled for what to do next. Kele and Akalei would arrive soon.

Changing direction, my dolphin friends torpedoed for the Seamount beach landing where Moho had taken me the first time I'd seen his new home. Sandy beaches stretched beneath a towering volcano, which puffed smoke from its simmering peak. I jogged up the trail to the caldera where I knew I could speak into the prison cell Moho kept in the soul room. He had kept me there not long before when I'd been his captive. It seemed the mostly likely place Moho would keep Kupua and for some reason it created a barrier to my ability to communicate, so I'd have to do it the old fashioned way.

Sweat sheened my neck and back as I huffed up the steep trail. From the top, I viewed the surrounding island. The beaches lay empty. Completely deserted of human life. Open sea as far as my eyes could see into the horizon, white caps dotting the surface like floating cotton swabs. Scrambling over the rocks and gravel, I slid to the spot where the ground had devoured me into the cell below the last time I had visited this barren landscape. "Kupua. Can you hear me?"

Silence. I raised my voice to a shout, cupping my hands around my mouth. "Kupua. Are you there?"

"Tessa. Yes. I'm here, in the soul room. What are you doing up there?"

"Waiting for Kele. We're going to rescue you. What's Moho doing?"

"He's arguing with Henry. He's saying something about needing a sacrifice. Tessa, I don't want you here. Please. Escaping from this room is not a problem for me but I need to wait for a chance to grab that spear. Get somewhere safe. I'll join you as soon as I can."

"You know better than that. We aren't leaving you. Kele's bringing rope and we can pull you out from above. We'll find another way to steal the spear. Just hang on."

"If you take me out now this will all be for nothing. Let's wait, see what happens. Maybe I can still get the spear. This is the best opportunity we may have for awhile."

I grumbled and kicked the gravel. "Ugh. I don't like this. Too much can go wrong."

"I love you Tessa. It will be okay. Besides, I have extra motivation. Nothing could keep me from our wedding."

I nodded my head, even though he couldn't see me and pressed fingers against my eyes to stop the tears threatening to spill. "I love you, too, Kupua, and I trust you. We'll wait. But, not too long, okay?"

"Deal."

I crossed my legs and plopped onto the gravel. I might be waiting, but I wasn't leaving. Not with Kupua's life at risk.

CHAPTER 11

MOHO

MOHAI

SACRIFICE

The soul room reeked of sulfur. Vapors brimming with the toxin wafted from the crack in the raised rock that led to the lair of the Lua Pele. Steam lingered in the air before dispersing and leaving its stench behind. The rock fissure served as an altar of sorts, used to deliver sacrifices to the evil harbored below. Positioned in front of the altar stood my throne. Bleached bones wove together to form its legs, seat and back. Remnants of victims too weak to overcome the power of the Lua Pele. The only other structure in the room was the cell that held my brother.

Time to keep your promise, Moho. Time for my sacrifice. The voice raked through my skull with the heat of hot coals. "I know." I groaned, pressing both hands against my forehead.

Henry squinted at me. "Who you talking to?"

"The Lua Pele requires a sacrifice and grows tired of waiting."

He cleared his throat and shifted slightly. "What kind of sacrifice?"

"A human sacrifice. It craves a life. Care to volunteer?"

He backed up a step and rubbed his hands together. "You're joking right?"

"No." I shifted my gaze to Kupua who sat with his back to us. "It wants my brother. Royal blood."

He released a sigh. "Well, that solves one of our problems."

Cold dread filled my chest. My stomach roiled as unfamiliar emotions churned. The flesh on my arms burned and tore as welts and slashes appeared. *No hesitation. You are mine. Do not forget.*

I pointed at Kupua. "Bring him to me."

Clear, sound proofed, plexi-glass walls surrounded Kupua, who sat cross-legged on the ground in human form. His bare chest glistened with sweat as his eyes followed my movements. Henry opened a small side door and jerked him to his feet. With both hands chained behind his back, Kupua would not be able to change shape. His chin lifted as he met my stare. "Congratulations, brother, I hear you are to become a father. We will welcome your child into our family."

I faltered at his words, my hand clutching my chest for a brief moment. My teeth ground together as I spoke. "Not your concern." Burning pain jabbed my sides.

No stalling. Give him to me.

Henry shoved Kupua onto his knees before my throne. His head bowed, my brother's shaggy brown hair clung to his neck with sweat and a slight tremble vibrated along his arms. "Fighting your bonds will do you no good brother, you cannot escape."

"Why are you doing this? What do you hope to accomplish?"

In one quick move, I snatched his arm and slammed him onto the edge of the fissure leading to the depths of the Lua Pele's lair. "Your blood is valuable to the Lua Pele. I pay my debts and this one is due. Prepare yourself. It's time for you to leave this world."

He squeezed his eyes shut against the steam vapors pouring from the crack. His hair stuck to his face from the humidity. "Even if you take my life, we will always be brothers. I forgive you, for everything. I will love you even beyond this existence on earth."

My heart shuddered. Memories flooded from childhood of Kupua and I exploring caves and riding ocean waves. I'd looked up to him as my big brother, even loved him once. Paralysis gripped me as emotions surged through my veins like soda being shaken in a bottle.

Do it now. Shove him into my lair. Stabs of burning pain bore into my side. I gasped. "I didn't ask for your forgiveness."

His voice rasped, a mere whisper. "I should have been there to protect you when your gift activated. I'm sorry. It wasn't your fault."

Images of that day clouded my vision, sharks responding to my anger and attacking my friend. I hadn't known how to control the sharks back then and things had gotten out of control. A feeding frenzy left my best friend dead, in pieces on the ocean floor. I'd been too ashamed to return home. It was the Lua Pele who had found me, sheltered me, taught me. Now it owned me.

End this, Moho. Blinding pain shot through my chest and my grip faltered. "I can't." My grip loosened and I sunk to my knees.

Kupua followed me to the ground, his hands still bound behind his back. "We will always be family. I love you, my brother."

Claws raked across my arms, ripping open my flesh. I reached around Kupua's back and unlocked his chains. My teeth clenched in agony as I spoke. "Leave now, before I change my mind and serve you to the monster."

No. You will not defy me.

"Get out…now!"

Kupua crouched nose to nose with me. "Come with me. I cannot leave you to this torment. We can fight it together. You aren't alone."

"No, we cannot. I must face this alone. Go or you'll not get a second chance."

Henry stalked closer and grabbed for Kupua. I held up a hand. "Do not stop him. I'm releasing him." Piercing heat scorched my chest as new slashes sliced through my skin. I curled into a ball and moaned against the pain.

We had a deal.

Kupua rose, his face twisted in sorrow. "You're strong, Moho, but ask the Creator to help you. Only he can break you free from this darkness. We'll all wait for your return." He spun and raced from the room. A piece of my soul broke, warring between anger and despair.

Henry sneered and swung at me, his eyes blazing with volcanic fire. "You weak fool." His fist grazed my chin and I sprang forward to tackle him. We landed with a thud against the hard floor.

"Stop. This is not your business. It's my choice to make." Gathering my feet beneath me, I stood and watched him rise, a snarl on his lips.

"You're ruining us." He gripped my arms and attempted to shove me against the wall, but I outweighed him and held my ground. Hunching over, I pummeled him with my shoulder and sent him reeling backwards. He stumbled, lost his balance and tumbled into the crack leading to the Lua Pele's lair. His hands shot forward as he screamed. "Help."

I leaped toward him to snatch his hand but it was too late. He vanished into a burst of steam and fire, sucked beyond my reach, trapped in the Lua Pele's grip.

Accepted.

Wounds along my arms and chest knit together and faded. I collapsed to my knees and sunk my face into my hands. Another life lost. He may have been born on the surface, but he was still family and my responsibility. Heaviness suffocated me as hopelessness clutched my soul.

A distant voice hummed in the background of my mind, warm and soft. *You are not alone. Call to me.*

CHAPTER 12

TESSA

MANA'OLANA

HOPE

"Tessa, I'm free and waiting on the shore." Kupua called to me through the mental path we shared. His voice slid through my mind with love and warmth. I burst down the trail at top speed, anxious to reassure myself he was really safe. Where sea lapped against sand, he stood, his shaggy hair framing his face. Dimples framed his lopsided smile. My heart skipped as joy blossomed in my chest and I threw my arms around his neck, nearly bowling him over.

He stumbled back a step. "Hey, it's okay. I'm safe."

I buried my nose in his neck and inhaled his sweet salty scent. "I love you."

He squeezed me tight until I felt the beat of his heart against mine. "I love you, too, Ipo. Sorry to scare you."

"I heard part of what went on. He planned on sacrificing you to the Lua Pele. His own brother. How could he be so cruel?"

"But he didn't. There's hope, Tessa. He released me. There's hope for my brother." He stroked my hair and I clung to him for several moments before loosening my grip and stepping back.

He brushed my cheek with his finger. "We'll figure out another way to get the spear. How about we go home and get ready for our wedding?"

Heat flashed my cheeks. "Sounds good to me."

We sliced through the water, me hugging Kupua's back as he jetted through the sea in dolphin form. Fin and his pod glided through the waves beside us, bursting above the surface in powerful leaps as they celebrated the end of the hurricane, which had calmed during Kupua's captivity. Guess Moho had what he wanted.

Kele and Akalei greeted us on the gravel beach of our home. "Thank the Creator you're home safe." Akalei wrapped her arms around me as I emerged, dripping, from the sea. Kele clapped hands with Kupua before yanking him into a bear hug. We all clung to each other, our bodies conveying the emotions we couldn't bear to speak. Finally, Akalei leaned back and examined my face. "Are you as exhausted as you look?"

"It shows? Things didn't go exactly as planned. I guess it took more out of me than I thought."

"Listen to Akalei." Kupua chimed in. Pointing at my friend, he added. "Take care of her and make sure she gets some rest."

"On it." She replied, and tucked me under her arm, practically dragging me to my bed, where I curled into a ball and fell asleep without argument.

Jasmine tea steeped somewhere close by, its enticing aroma coaxing my eyelids open. I grumbled and rolled to my side, scanning the room for its source. Akalei sat with her toes in the moat surrounding my bed, with a cup and saucer by her side. "Is that for me or are you being a tease?"

She grinned and scooped up the cup, stepped over the moat and handed it to me, before plopping on the edge of my bed. I sat up and sipped the steamy goodness, relishing the warmth as it slid down my throat. Akalei watched me like a cat who'd just swallowed a mouse. I squinted at her. "What?"

"I know the wedding's officially planned for next week but your sister and I decided to move it up. I mean, with the way things go around here why risk putting it off, right?"

"What do you mean, moved it up?" My stomach did a little flip. Akalei bit her lip and avoided my gaze.

"Don't freak out." She scooted away from me.

"Saying don't freak out…makes me freak out."

She threw her palms up in front of her as if to hold me back. "Surprise. You're getting married today!"

My breath caught and tingles spread through my chest. It's not like I didn't want to get married, I did, but had expected to have a few days to prepare myself.

"Tessa, say something."

"What…How? Why?"

"Rachel and I needed something to do while you were gone, so we got everything ready early. It was therapeutic. Are you mad?"

"No, I'm not mad. Just adjusting. When I woke up, I didn't think I'd be getting married today. My thoughts flashed to Kupua. "Does Kupua know?"

She winced. "Kele and Mike are telling him now."

I giggled and set my cup on the floor. "Love to hear that conversation."

Rachel burst into the room, my wedding dress draped in her arms. She'd cut her hair and it bobbed around her shoulders with a slight curl at the ends. Her eyes shone as she gently laid the dress on the bed and leaned down to kiss my cheek. "I assume Akalei has brought you up to speed with our plans. Isn't it exciting? I just wish mom and dad could be here, Sis."

Tears pressed against my eyes. "Me, too." I choked out and ducked my head. "Don't make me cry, my face will get all puffy and I'll look like a puffer fish at my wedding."

"You're going to look gorgeous, but not if we don't start getting you ready." Akalei hopped to her feet, flung the covers off my lap and clapped her hands. "Up…up."

After several hours of primping and plucking, I stood before a mirror in awe at the results. My hair was braided with strands of tiny pearls and piled on my head with loose wisps curling around my face. A shear, pale green veil cascaded from the crown on my head to my waist. A strand of black pearls wrapped around my neck, hanging above the sweetheart neckline of my dress. Layers of ankle length tulle dotted with flecks of mother of pearl puffed from my waist. A sash of chiffon, braided with beads made from the same mother of pearl tied in a bow at my back. Glitter sparkled on my feet and toes, catching the light like twinkling stars. "Wow."

Rachel stood behind me and rested her chin on my shoulder,

meeting my gaze in the mirror. "You're so beautiful." She hugged me tight. "I'm gonna cry."

"Don't you dare," Akalei chimed. "We don't have time to re-do anyone's make-up."

I spun to inspect their dresses. Akalei wore purple, the formal color of the royal guard. Both she and Kele had accepted the honored position with the guard when I had been crowned. A halter of chiffon circled her neck in layers and hung to the hem above her knees.

Green satin with an empire waist flattered my sister's post baby shape and she radiated contentment. A garland of tiny Kings Crown conch shells adorned her neck. "I love you both." I spread my arms wide around them as I choked back the lump clogging my throat.

"Wait, I have something for you." Rachel jogged to her pile of clothing and retrieved a small package, returning with a shy smile on her face and a twinkle in her eyes. She stretched out her arm and nudged the gift into my hand. "It's from mom. She did this just after you were born. I found one for you and me in the safe after she died."

My fingers shook as I untied the bow and opened the box. A pair of diamond earrings lay inside and tucked underneath was a folded note. I carefully plucked it from the box and opened it.

Tessa. My baby. You are so tiny in my arms it's hard to imagine one day you will be a grown woman. I wanted to capture my thoughts now, to share with you on the day you leave your father and I, to start a family of your own. First, never doubt how much we love you. You are a precious gift and have brought so much joy into our lives. Second, I have some motherly advice for your wedding day. Forgive. Every day, forgive. Don't hold any grudge or bitterness in your heart. Love with abandon. Just as your father and I love you, sweetie, Mom

Tears rolled silently down my cheeks. Immobilized, hesitant to part with the note and break the fragile connection to my mom, every muscle stilled. Rachel laid her hand on my arm. "She's always with us."

I nodded, handed her the note and scooped out the earrings. "They're so beautiful." After securing them on my earlobes I twirled on my toes. "I'm ready. Let's do this."

Hand in hand, we walked through the palace, our steps light, as if we floated on clouds of joy. When we reached the steps that led down to the sacred pool, my chest fluttered. My city spread out below, like a rare jewel, glistening in candlelight. Lanterns flickered on the still water of the pool like stars in the sky. Birds of Paradise lined the polished abalone streets, potted in volcanic rock containers. People gathered on one end of the pool, sitting on levels of raised benches which several of the men in the city had recently built at Kele's request. On the opposite end of the pool my ocean friends jockeyed for position in a mass of sea lions, monk seals and sea turtles. Lizzy lumbered to where we stood, a braided strand of sea kelp adorning her neck. I leaned over and accepted her slimy kiss on my cheek. "Love you, Lizzy."

She barked and slapped her flipper against the polished floor. Slowly, we descended the steep staircase. At the bottom, I paused to absorb the scene.

Sitting on the edge of the sacred pool, Mike strummed his guitar, his gentle melody setting a peaceful tone in the city. Kupua perched beside him, a huge grin plastered on his face as he caught my gaze. My heart skipped. He wore a green tunic, embroidered with mother of pearl to match my dress. A crown of pearl, matching my own, circled his head. Rachel and Akalei released my hands and I rushed to his side and clasped his hands.

"You're shaking." He whispered in my ear, his warm breath caressing my neck.

"I know. Can't seem to stop."

"Scared?"

"No. Excited. Happy. Let's do this."

He twined his arm around mine and turned us toward the water. About a foot beneath the surface a platform hung suspended in the clear blue sea. It would allow us to speak our vows while partially immersed in the ocean that we so passionately protected. Lizzy slid into the pool and claimed her place next to mine on the platform. Kupua lead me down the steps and into the warmth of the sea, keeping a strong grip on my hand. Ka coasted to Kupua's side and gave him a playful nip on the leg. Kupua ran his free hand along her glistening shell and I felt her love for him echo in my own heart. They'd been friends her whole life.

We faced each other on the platform and held tight to one another's hands. Every nerve in my body hummed, strung tight with anticipation like a wound up jack in the box ready to pop.

Kupua cleared his throat and spoke, his voice unwavering. "I give my love to you. Aloha aku nô. I pledge eternal Aloha to you, my queen. From this moment forward you shall not walk alone. I promise to honor, cherish and respect you. I give you my strength. Together, we will work as one for our Creator to protect His oceans. I will love you forever, aloha au ai oa mauloa."

Tears spilled down my cheeks and I swallowed a lump of emotion as my heart melted into mushy goo. Kupua slid the green coral ring onto my finger and leaned forward to kiss my hand. Straightening, his eyes locked onto mine and filled me with the heat of a simmering volcano. I sniffed and gathered myself, lifting my chin. "I give my love to you and pledge eternal Aloha to you, my king. From this moment forward you shall not walk alone. I promise to honor, cherish and respect you. My heart is yours. I give you my strength. My hopes and dreams I trust in your care. Together, we will work as one for our Creator to protect His oceans. I will love you forever, aloha au ai oa mauloa." His hand trembled as I slipped a matching green coral ring onto his finger.

Kele and Akalei joined us in the water, holding hands and grinning ear to ear. Kele slapped his hand onto the surface, splashing us both in the face. With a chuckle, he lifted his voice so the gathered crowd could easily hear. "No gift is more valuable than love. Akalei and I bear witness to the words spoken here and promise to support and nurture this marriage. E kolu mea nui, Ame kealoha kealoha kai oi ahe, po maikai, na mea apau, the greatest things in life are faith, hope and love, but the greatest of these three is love." They both bowed their heads. "We serve the Creator. We submit to your authority as king and queen, appointed by our Creator. We commit our love and loyalty to you and your children." As he raised his head, I caught the glint of tears pressing against Kele's eyes. He winked at me before diving with Akalei into the pool and emerging under the waterfall, their arms raised in celebration.

Kupua nodded in their direction. "Ready?"

"Always."

We followed our friends, submitting to the pounding water as it beat our heads and accepted the blessings of the crowd which now thundered its approval. Sea lions barked and dove into the pool, swarming us with congratulations. Flippers splashed against the water's surface as they expressed their excitement. I wrapped one arm around Lizzy and kissed her head before Kupua tugged me to the edge of the pool and boosted me onto land. Immediately, my dress dried, the special material made by Eka's family demonstrating its legendary quality. Rachel and Mike plowed into me, embracing both Kupua and I with their love. The crowd pressed against us, each person shouting congratulations until we lost ourselves to the tangled mass of affection.

Muscles in my face cramped from smiling for three hours straight. Kupua steered me toward a private corner near the waterfall. He brushed my cheek with his lips and circled my waist with his arms. "How about we ditch this party and start our honeymoon?

I rested my head against his chest. "Now, please."

He chuckled. "Kele's going to cover for us so we can slip away to the Queen's Chamber. Remember the last time you were there?"

I nodded and smiled up at him. I'd spent the night there before my crowning. Its location was known only to the king, queen and royal guard. Hidden, not far from the city, but easily accessed through secret lava tube tunnels. "This time I won't be alone."

"And then you can choose the destination of your choice for our own private escape. A real honeymoon."

I pushed him back a step and grabbed his hand. "Come on, let's get out of here."

We slunk behind the waterfall and dove into the pool, navigating toward our destination.

When we reached the Queen's Chamber I stretched out my hands and placed them on the door, holding my breath as it opened. Kupua swept me into his arms and lifted me over the threshold. Inside, candles lit the room. The far wall a clear sheet of glass through which we could view all the wonders of the ocean outside, but none could see within. Coral spread from the ocean floor in vibrant orange, pink and green explosions of color. Tiny fish darted in and out of sight with bursts of speed.

Kupua set my feet on the cool polished floor, but I remained ensconced in his arms, relishing the smell of ocean on his skin. He buried his face in my neck and took a deep breath of his own. "I love you, Tessa."

My eyes closed as I leaned into him. "I love you too, my king."

He brushed my cheek with his lips. "Are you hungry?"

A giggle escaped my lips. "You read my mind."

He spun me to face a white marble table piled with strawberries and chocolate. After popping one in my mouth and sighing with pleasure, I snatched another from the platter and held it in the air with a wink in Kupua's direction. "Come closer."

He leaned into me, his lips parted as I slid the fruit into his mouth. My fingers lingered, tracing the contours of his jaw. He stilled, his gaze fixed on mine with one eyebrow raised. "Maybe I'm not so hungry after all."

CHAPTER 13

TESSA

PU

TOGETHER

Light filtered into the room as morning broke and the sun cast its rays through the ocean depths. A purple striped jellyfish propelled past our window to the sea. Its long stingers drifted with the current, likely in search of zooplankton for breakfast. I curled onto my side and snuggled closer to Kupua's warmth. He yawned and whispered into my hair. "Good morning, my wife. You smell delicious."

"Really? What do I smell like? Bacon?" I giggled into his neck.

"More like honey drizzled over a sugar cookie. You are sweet to the core."

I shoved against his chest. "You're either still asleep or a horrible flirt."

His eyes widened in mock shock. "What? You don't believe me? I'm totally serious. You doubt I think you are sweet?"

"Let's just say I was hoping for strong and powerful."

"Tessa, you can be strong, powerful and sweet. In fact, they balance each other well. You are the perfect queen, strong and kind." He squeezed me and changed the subject. "Have you decided where you want to go for our honeymoon?"

My eyebrows scrunched together. "Maybe we shouldn't go anywhere. I mean, I'd love to, but Moho's still out there with the spear and we're needed at home. He's bound to use it again and we need to be ready."

"We'll always be needed at home, but there's nothing that cannot wait for our return. Kele and Akalei can look after things in our absence and send word if there is trouble. Taking time to focus on us and our new marriage is more important right now."

"Maybe, but what if Moho uses the spear?"

"You didn't see Moho when he set me free. He's fighting the Lua Pele's hold. He did it, Tessa. He made the right choice even though it cost him terribly. He's changing."

"I hope you're right. You know I haven't given up on him being restored to our family. But isn't that all the more reason to stick close?"

He sighed and pressed his lips to my hand. "No. Grant me this request, my queen, and agree to leave our cares behind and spend some time together."

My heart melted and tingles shot up my arm. "You don't play fair."

He smiled and kissed my wrist, working his way up my arm. "Your answer?"

"Yes. My answer is yes. How can I refuse you?"

His mouth quirked to one side. "Good. Now, where are we going?"

"Hmmm…I've always wanted to see the Great Barrier Reef. What do you think?"

"Great idea. It'll take a few days to get there, but I've got a surprise that will help us along the way."

I squirmed under his touch. "A surprise? When did you have time to put together another surprise?"

He wagged his eyebrows. "I have my ways."

"Come on. Tell me what it is."

He rolled and hopped onto the floor. "How about I show you and we start our adventure now?"

Groaning, I covered my face with my hands. "Do we have to get up?"

"Do you want to see the surprise or not?"

Pushing myself into a sitting position, I waved at him. "All right. You win."

He tossed a short green wetsuit my way and shoved a leg into his own. "Put this on. We don't want our queen to get cold on her honeymoon."

"Are you expecting colder waters?"

"Only if we have to go deeper, just to be safe. If we travel farther below, we're less likely to run into any surface dwellers."

Stifling a grumble, I shimmied soft fabric up my legs and over my arms. It did feel cozy and warm against my skin. Sliding off the bed, I narrowed my eyes at my new husband. "Okay. Ready. Where's the surprise?"

"Patience." He strode to the door and opened it with a sweep of his arm. "This way, my queen."

I sidled up to him and whispered in his ear. "This better be worth leaving that comfy bed."

Confidence pooled in his eyes. "Oh, I think you're going to appreciate this surprise."

Through the door lay the short corridor to the submerged volcanic tubes that lead to open ocean. As we slipped into the sea, he covered my eyes with his hands. "Now just wait a minute." My back pressed against his chest and I savored the warmth that flowed from his heart into mine. My husband.

A whoosh of current brushed past my face. "What was that?"

"Not yet. Another minute or two and everything will be in place."

I could hear squeals and chirps from dolphins nearby and reached out with my hands but my fingers traced through empty water. Kupua released his grip and announced. "For you, my love."

Hovering a few feet before me was a small submarine like carriage pulled by six members of my favorite dolphin family with Fin at the lead. Expansive windows formed the front, back and sides of the shiny blue and green sub. Strands of kelp connected the sub to the dolphins, who held the leafy ends in their mouths. I spun to face Kupua. "Where did you find this?"

He wrapped an arm around my shoulder. “Remember that submarine we rescued for the surface dwellers?”

I nodded. Whales had helped us raise it from the depths so surface dwellers could locate it.

“Well…it got me thinking about how we might borrow the idea and create our own transportation for longer trips. Is it worthy of my queen?”

“It’s perfect.” I kissed his cheek. “How do we get inside?”

“Ah. Let me show you.” He clasped my hand and we swam underneath the sub where he spun a wheel and unlocked a pressurized chamber. Raising my arms, I pulled myself inside and sat on the seat against the metal wall while Kupua did the same. He yanked the latch shut, twisting a wheel attached to the inside of the door. Its whine echoed in the small space as it sealed. A boom sounded and above our heads another door opened into the main cabin of the submarine.

As I squeezed through the small entry and straightened in the cabin, a gasp escaped my lips. A mural of my life adorned the walls of the interior. The image of my sister and her husband smiled at me with their home on Lanai in the background. On the far side of the cabin, my parents’ faces greeted me, their images taken from a cherished Christmas photo tucked away in one of the few books I’d brought to Moku-ola. Splashed across the ceiling my sea friends, Lizzy, Sid, Rico and Kupua’s Ka danced. “Who painted this? It’s amazing.”

“Eka created this before she left. We’ve been working on it for a while. It wasn’t easy keeping the secret from you.”

"Wow. She's so talented." Tears pressed against my eyes and I turned and threw my arms around his neck. "Thank you. This gift is incredible."

He stroked my hair. "It's nothing compared to the gift you've given me."

I pulled back and frowned at him. "But I haven't given you anything. In fact, I'm feeling a little like a slacker right now."

His eyes lit with a sparkle. "Agreeing to be queen and share your life with me in the sea is the most precious gift I could ever ask for. Thank you, Tessa, for your courage and love."

A lump formed in the back of my throat. Words failed to capture my heart. I hugged my king tight and allowed our bond to express all the emotions welling within me. After several moments, I released him. "Who gets to drive?"

He chuckled. "You do, of course."

I skipped to the front where two plush leather captain chairs waited. Slipping into the one on the left, I examined the brightly lit control panel. "Okay, what first?"

He settled into the chair next to me and raised an eyebrow. "You don't actually think those work do you?"

Heat flushed my cheeks as my mind clicked. "Oh….right. The dolphins. I just need to tell them where to go."

"To the Great Barrier Reef."

CHAPTER 14

TESSA

KUPAIANAHA MAKAI

WONDERFUL OCEAN

We hid the sub in the depths surrounding the Australian reef and thanked Fin and his family for their service. Hand in hand, Kupua and I kicked to the shallower waters ready to explore the underwater terrain. Two sea snakes, Claude and Westeria, met us on our ascent and welcomed us to their waters, serving as escort as we swam. The ocean teemed with trumpet, clown and striped surgeonfish who flitted in and around coral. Sunlight filtered in shafts of light reflecting off their bright colors like a rainbow kaleidoscope.

Urgent whispers called my name and I adjusted my course to respond. Giant clams fringed the reef and invited me closer. Each one measured about 50 inches wide, with bright green, blue and gold striped patterns adorning their muscles. When open, their muscles stretched out several feet like decorated tongues waiting for morsels to land. The eldest clam requested an audience. *Welcome Queen of the Seas. Will you come speak with us?*

I bowed my head in acknowledgement of one much older than I.

Please help us. Humans are taking many of our members away and our numbers are dangerously low. We need your assistance. Will you help us? Can you stop this?

"Who is doing this and when do they come?" I inquired.

Surface dwellers arrive at dusk, when we close for the night.

"As your queen, you have my protection. I promise to do what is within my power."

A sigh of relief wafted through my senses and compassion tugged my heart. Kupua touched my arm. "What do you plan to do?"

"We have to find a way to discourage these offenders from stealing our friends. Giant clams are considered a protected species on dry land, so whoever is taking them is breaking the law."

"Obviously, they don't care about the law and not too many patrols travel out this remotely to catch them."

"Where are we, exactly?"

"Close to Haggerstone Island. There's about 2900 individual reef systems that make up the Great Barrier Reef and we're as remote as you can get so we don't have to worry about being noticed." He winked. "Plus, I hoped for some privacy with my new bride."

Heat flushed my cheeks. Being referred to as his bride still seemed so foreign to me. "Sorry…seems duty beckons."

He twined his fingers in mine. "Never apologize. We're in this together. We could never turn our backs on our subjects in their time of need."

Warmth curled around my heart and drenched me in his love. "I have an idea."

"Of course you do."

Several hours later, Kupua and I waited, concealed behind an outcropping of rocks and coral within sight of the giant clams. Our plan was ready. As darkness dropped its veil across the sea, my skin tingled with anticipation.

Splashing at the surface provided the first clue our poachers were near. Shafts of light pierced the darkness and we caught a glimpse of two divers toting a mesh bag behind them. Anger boiled in my chest at the thought of their intent. Kupua's hand rested on my shoulder, soothing and calming my emotions. I covered his hand with mine. "Thank you."

One of the divers paused next to the clam I'd spoken with earlier, knife in hand, he motioned the other to join him. My gut wrenched. As the divers positioned themselves around the clam a dozen sea snakes slithered from their hiding places beneath the shells, their bodies curling and stretching toward the human interlopers. Bubbles exploded from the divers as their arms cartwheeled in retreat. Sea snake poison could kill a grown surface dweller before he even had a chance to reach air. The snakes hovered between the divers and the clams as if possessively staking their claim. One diver attempted to approach the clams from another direction, only to be faced with another wall of slithering, protective snakes.

Finally, the divers gave up and slowly kicked to the surface. A sigh of relief escaped my lips. Kupua squeezed my shoulder. "Your plan worked."

"Yeah. For now. I think the snakes are going to have to keep watch on a permanent basis."

Bubbles floated from the mouths of the clams. *Thank you Queen Tessa. You have saved us.*

"You are welcome. The snakes will continue to guard you. Be well my friends."

Kupua tugged my arm. "Come on, let's get some rest. We've got a honeymoon to continue in the morning."

As the sun rose over the horizon the next morning, Kupua and I swam ashore on Haggerstone Island. Silky white sand cushioned my feet as I stood and relished the sun warming my cheeks. Kupua twined his fingers in mine.

"I thought you might enjoy some surface time."

"It's perfect."

His mouth quirked to one side. "Oh, there's more."

I raised an eyebrow. "Is there no end to your surprises?"

"You'll see." He tugged my hand and we strolled along the edge of the surf.

Warm water lapped my ankles as waves rolled in against the shore. Fresh salty air filled my lungs, and with each exhale, I relaxed a little bit more. Kupua steered me over a sand dune to discover a hidden fresh water lagoon nestled among rock boulders and lush green vegetation. A blanket lay atop a patch of sandy grass, adorned with fresh fruit and two goblets of sparkling water.

Kupua bowed, sweeping his hand. "Your breakfast, my Ipo."

I rose to my tiptoes to kiss his cheek, but he wrapped his arm around my waist and pressed his lips against mine. He tasted of salty sea and home, melting my heart with the warmth of his love. The kiss ended too soon and I lingered in his embrace. "You were right. I really needed this getaway."

"I'll always look out for you, my love."

"Do you think we'll ever have peace?"

"Peace comes from a right relationship with our Creator, not with the world. We already have it." He tapped his heart. "Don't let our enemies steal what does not belong to them."

The truth of his words stirred my spirit. "You're right. All this time I've blamed Moho for my stress, but it's been my choice to allow him to get under my skin. No more." I sighed. "Thank you for always knowing how to make me feel better."

"We must do that for each other. Now…no more talk of Moho. This is our escape, remember?"

"Right. Let's eat."

He released his hold on my waist and I skipped to the blanket and nestled into the comfort of sand and sun. Kupua plopped on his stomach and elbows before snatching a chunk of pineapple off the platter. Next to him, I lay on my back, hands behind my head and soaked in warmth as well as his words like a sponge. He dropped a grape into my mouth. It's juicy sweetness trickled down my throat.

"I might have an idea about how to get the spear."

His eyebrows scrunched together. “Stop.” He dropped another grape into my mouth before I could speak. “Honeymoon, remember?

I grunted and swallowed the grape. “I can’t help it. My thoughts keep going back to keeping everyone safe.”

He sat up. “Flip over.”

“Why?”

“Just do it. Trust me.”

“Fine.” I rolled onto my stomach.

“Now close your eyes.”

My chest expanded as I took a deep breath and shut out the world. Birds chirped from the branches of a nearby tree, a sweet lullaby for my rest. Kupua’s fingers prodded the muscles along my neck and shoulders, squeezing out tension as he massaged. A groan of pleasure escaped my lips and he chuckled, but didn’t slow his pursuit of loosening the grip of stress on my body. He rolled his fist across my back. Muscles shifted and eased under his touch. I drifted into that peaceful place between waking and sleep. When I finally opened my eyes, the sun was high in the sky. “Did I fall asleep?”

“Yup. Slept half the day away.”

“Why’d you let me do that?”

“Why not? You have someplace to go?”

I scrambled to my knees and flicked his arm. “Funny.”

"Ouch. Testy, aren't we? Seems a nap wasn't enough." He sprang to his feet. "Follow me. There's something you'll want to see."

Tall grass tickled my bare skin as we traipsed across an open field. Shrubs exploding with purple blossoms scented the air with flora sweetness. Kupua lead me over a small cluster of boulders to another secluded lagoon of crystal clear seawater. He plopped onto the sand and patted the spot next to him. "Join me while we wait."

"Wait for what?"

"The surprise, what else?"

Sand cocooned me with its warmth as I settled beside Kupua. Seagulls glided overhead and called out greetings before sailing over open ocean. Peace curled around me as all demands faded away in the face of the island's solitude. "It is nice here."

Kupua slipped his hand in mine, keeping his gaze on the lagoon. "Life isn't always about doing things. Sometimes it's about rest and restoration. This time is just as important as anything else we might do."

"How did you get so wise?"

He shrugged. "I just listen to the Creator and trust him."

"Well, thank you for making me listen to you. I needed this more than I realized."

"You didn't make it easy."

"Yeah, sorry about that."

He lifted a finger to his mouth and pointed to a spot a few feet from where we sat. My gaze shifted and I sucked in a breath. Tiny flippers and heads poked through the silky white sand as dozens of baby green sea turtles emerged from their nest ready to scramble toward the beckoning surf. "Aw…they're so cute," I whispered as I crawled closer, carefully placing one hand in front of the other. Bodies the size of quarters flopped about as they wriggled forward. Seagulls gathered overhead until I blasted them with an order to stand down. "No babies for you today." With a light tap of my finger, I flipped one who'd stranded himself on his back and giggled as he scurried away. I glanced over my shoulder. "How did you know they were here?"

"Ka told me where to look before we left. This is a favorite spot for green sea turtles to lay eggs. When you were asleep, I scoped it out."

Ka was a sea turtle with unshakable loyalty to Kupua. She'd been by his side since boyhood. "Make sure to thank Ka for me."

"Consider it her wedding gift to us."

I crept beside the tiny creatures as they scrambled into the surf and took their first ocean plunge. They bobbed like tiny balls until ducking beneath the waves and disappearing. I flashed a smile over my shoulder at Kupua. "Best gift ever."

When all the babies had made their way into the sea, Kupua and I laid back on the blanket and stared into the sky until the stars came out. We marveled as the horizon darkened from blue to black. A star flashed across the sky in a burst of light before extinguishing. "Quick, make a wish Kupua."

"A wish?"

"Yes. On the surface they wish on falling stars. What do you wish for?"

"I don't believe in wishes. It takes faith and action to make your dreams and wishes come true."

"Well, then tell me your greatest dream. What do you want to take action on to make happen?"

His chest rose and fell. I waited. "There is only one missing piece in my life right now. The one thing that I, alone, cannot change. To have my brother back and restored to our family. But, this requires him to take action. He must want it as well. No amount of wishing will change his mind. I ask myself every day if I am doing enough, if there is something I have missed that might make a difference. His face haunts my dreams. The hole he left in my heart yearns for his return."

His pain lanced my heart and silent tears tracked down my cheeks. I twisted to my side and propped my head up on my hand to examine his face. Moonlight cast shadows under his eyes, marking the sorrow weighing on his features. I leaned over and softly pressed my lips against his. Tentative at first, until his hand wrapped behind my neck and the gentleness gave sway to the fire burning within our hearts. We clung to one another as sorrow transformed into passion and the night took a different turn.

CHAPTER 15

TESSA

MANA'O

IDEA

Five days later, I leaned back against the plush seat in our sub and sighed. "Remind me again, why are we leaving?"

Kupua chuckled. "Weren't you the one complaining about being away too long?"

"You must have me confused with the stressed out Queen of Moku-ola. I'm the relaxed, carefree woman who just spent a week playing with her new husband."

He reached out and squeezed my hand. "Hold onto that feeling as long as you can."

Fin and his family launched us toward home, and as the ocean whizzed past my window, I tucked the memory of my time at the reef into a special corner of my brain to be pulled out later and cherished. With a deep breath, I gave Kupua a sideways glance. Locks of hair fell across his forehead and tangled with thick dark lashes. His smile, framed by matching dimples, warmed me from the inside out. My heart was no longer my own. It belonged to this man and I knew with the certainty of the tides, he would always be by my side. The knowledge steadied me like an anchor with a ship in the currents.

A thud on the front window startled me from my reverie. Sid's tentacles splayed across the glass and exposed his beak, which tapped against the window. He had urgent news to report. I leaned to press my nose against the cool surface. "What's wrong?"

Forgive me, my queen, but this could not wait. A dangerous whirlpool has appeared and it is growing. There is a threat to ships as well as sea life. We've never seen anything like it.

"You did the right thing by finding me. Thank you, my friend. Now go home and let Kele and Akalei know we are on the way. We will find a way to deal with this new threat."

The suction cups on his tentacles released their grip and curled, then extended as he propelled away from the sub. An inky cloud puffed in his wake as he headed home.

"This has Moho written all over it. I knew he wouldn't wait long to use that spear. What do you think he hopes to gain from this whirlpool thing?"

"It could be a distraction."

"Well, even if it is we have to deal with it. We can't allow our problems to impact the surface world. If ships start to go down, then surface dwellers are going to be all over the area. We also need to gain control of the spear. I have an idea that might take care of both."

He quirked an eyebrow. "I'm listening."

What is the one thing Moho cares about?"

"Power."

"Besides power."

He closed his eyes. "His unborn child."

"Exactly. We can use those emotions to our advantage. If he believed the whirlpool posed a threat to Eka and the baby, he would act and all we have to do is be prepared."

"But Eka is with him and the whirlpool is nowhere near Seamount."

"They don't have to actually be in danger. He just needs to think they are."

"How do you propose to pull that off?"

"With a little help from our friends and your amazing camouflage skills."

He flashed his dimples at me. "I like the way your mind works."

My cheeks warmed. "Let's hope Moho takes the bait."

Once back in Moku-ola I laid out the details of my plan for Kupua, Kele and Akalei. Everyone agreed to implement phase one first thing in the morning. I prayed to the Creator it would go well.

CHAPTER 16

TESSA

HO'OLALA

PLAN

Kupua, now in the form of a blue shark, patrolled the entrance to Moho's lair, doing his best to mask the worry pinging through his thoughts, without much success. His sleek form flashed as he sliced through water. My heart drummed in my chest as I waited for his signal. It didn't take long. Moho exited his home on the back of Nikko. The two moved as one as they dove into the dark depths beyond the surrounding reef. When they disappeared from view, I slid into Seamount to search for Eka.

The heat and steam of the soul room triggered memories and sent shudders down my spine. Today it lay empty. No spear, no screams, just the oppressive blanket of air, which choked me with despair. I quickened my pace to the hall I hoped led to Eka's room. A cool breeze blew through the corridor, dropping the temperature, and allowing my breaths to deepen. Torches hung from the rock wall and flickered as I rushed past. An iron door, hung slightly ajar on my right. I leaned against it and listened, but no sound met my ears. Frowning, I peeked inside and spotted Eka with her back to me, sitting at a desk totally engrossed in her work. I rapped on the door and squeezed inside. Her head popped up and swerved to face me. "Queen Tessa." She cried and attempted to rise to her feet but the fullness of her pregnancy slowed her movement. Her stomach looked as if she'd swallowed a basketball. With one hand around her mid-section, she teetered toward me.

"Eka, you've gotten so big."

She ducked her head and smiled. "I know. The baby's due any day."

I strode forward and wrapped her in my arms, hugging her against me. "I've missed you."

"I've missed you too, but I'm happy here with Moho. You shouldn't have come. He'll be back soon and you know that won't end well for either of us."

"I only wanted to check on you and make sure you're okay. Please consider having lunch with me on the surface, just to catch up. We can leave Moho a note so he knows you're fine and will be right back."

She bit her lip and stepped away from me. "I'm not sure that's a good idea. Moho will get mad. He worries about me with the birth so close."

"You need some girlfriend time. You're all alone here and I have so much to tell you. We won't go far."

She wrung her hands and shifted her weight between legs. "I do miss talking to you and it does get lonely here." Her tone turned defensive. "But Moho's been so sweet and he's always making sure I have everything I need. Even today, he only left because I had a craving."

"He should be treating you well. You deserve to be loved and cared for Eka. Supporting your friendships is part of taking care of you, too. If he's so understanding, then he'll be okay with us spending time together."

"But he doesn't trust you and says I shouldn't either."

"Have I ever harmed you in any way?"

Her eyes shifted to her hands. "No. I guess it'll be okay, but just a quick lunch. Promise you'll make sure I'm back in an hour before he returns, so he won't have to worry."

I nodded. "We'll make it quick." I gazed around the room. "What about Henry? Will he be checking on you?"

She frowned. "Henry's no longer with us. He fell into that crack in the soul room. Moho says he's with the Lua Pele now." She shuddered. "That thing is awful."

I gasped. "How? When?"

"The day Kupua escaped. Moho had promised to sacrifice Kupua and when that didn't happen the Lua Pele took Henry instead. Moho says he had no choice. I never liked Henry but I wouldn't wish that on anyone."

A lump formed in my throat and my stomach churned with a swirl of anger, disbelief, sorrow and fear. "He wanted to send Kupua to the Lua Pele? His own brother?"

Eka backed up a step. "He couldn't go through with it. He allowed Kupua to escape instead. He's different. Kinder. I know he doesn't want to hurt anyone."

"But he planned to, and he betrayed Henry. I didn't like the guy either but he had a brother who loved him just like we love Moho." Poor Sam. A chill spread through my heart as I realized I'd have to give him the news. He was Henry's twin and he lived on Catalina Island.

"It wasn't Moho's choice, Tessa. The Lua Pele took Henry, not Moho. That thing is evil."

"There's always a choice involved, Eka. Moho is not innocent in this."

"Maybe we shouldn't do lunch. This is too upsetting and Moho says I should stay calm for the baby."

I shook off my emotions and focused. "No. I'm sorry. It was just a shock to hear about Henry. We won't talk about it anymore. Just good news."

Her eyes narrowed. "Are you sure?"

"Yes. Write your note to Moho and let's not waste anymore time."

With a shrug, she leaned over her desk and jotted a few words onto one of her sheets of paper.

I held out my hand for it. "I brought some sticky plant so we could put it on the door where he's sure not to miss it."

She slid it into my palm and waddled out the door. I slipped it into my pack and plucked out the note I'd prepared earlier, tacking it onto the door jam instead. A twinge of guilt stabbed at me. If there had been another way to convince Moho, I would have taken it.

She glanced over her shoulder. "I am getting hungry."

"Good. I've got a picnic all set up for you waiting on the beach." I followed her out and sent Kupua a signal that our plan was on target through our mental connection. Hopefully, phase two would go as smoothly.

CHAPTER 17

MOHO

I'NO

STORM

A chill shivered through me. Scooping the final sea cucumber into my pouch, I patted Nikko's side feeling an urgent need to speed home. My legs and arms wrapped around the thick torso of my shark as he sliced through currents like a torpedo. The Weather Spear clutched against my side and ready to be used if needed. Eka was too far along in her pregnancy to be left alone for more than a few minutes. If she hadn't begged for the delicacies in my bag, I wouldn't have considered traveling so far from Seamount. Her cravings were increasing as her due date approached.

Unease tickled my senses as the scent of an unknown shark filtered through the waters near the entrance to my home. A quick scan of the area failed to reveal the new predator. I surged off Nikko's back and kicked through the hidden passage before emerging inside Seamount. My heart beat against my chest when traces of Tessa's scent flared through my nostrils. A growl escaped my throat and my legs burst into a run toward Eka's chambers. Just outside her door hung a note written in Tessa's handwriting. I yanked it from the wall.

Moho, Eka is not in danger. Kupua and I would never harm her. We love both of you. The whirlpool you created is growing larger and destroying everything in its path. Meet us there, remove the threat and we will return Eka to your care. Queen Tessa.

Anger surged through my chest as I crumpled the paper and let it drop to the floor. A new emotion tangled itself around my heart- fear for Eka and our child. Despite what the letter stated, if she was near the funnel, Eka was in danger. Her pregnancy was too far along to risk taking her anywhere. Tessa would pay for this violation. Swerving on my heel, I raced to the sea gripping the spear as if it was now my only lifeline of hope.

Within moments, I careened west toward the maelstrom I'd created with my spear. Sharks swarmed on either side of Nikko and I and my emotions sparked like hot wires between us. As one, we rode currents, rolling and gliding in harmony with the surrounding water. Thoughts of Eka scorched my mind as every second that ticked by did not bring enough progress for my liking.

Currents strengthened and threatened to pull us off course, a sign we approached the whirlpool I'd created. Turbulence charged the sea, spinning and whipping kelp and other small debris in different directions. Jellyfish tumbled past us, rolling on the riptide like small tumbleweeds in a dust storm.

From the depths an orca emerged, within my sight but just out of striking distance. Anger flared at my brother and I raised the spear above my head. "Where is Eka?"

White light flashed and Kupua hovered in the water, no longer in Orca form. "Not until you calm this storm."

"I need to know she is safe and not hurt."

"You have my word, brother. Tessa and I would not put her at risk."

"Liar. You put her in danger by taking her from her home when she is about to give birth. Make no mistake, if any harm comes to her, I will destroy you and all you love, including your queen. Now bring her to me."

Sharks swarmed in a circle around Kupua and he threw his arms out in front of him. "Think, brother. We did not bring her here because the danger was too great. She's safe and as soon as you use the spear to stop this destructive funnel, I'll tell you where she is."

My nostrils flared as a blue shark struck at Kupua and tore flesh from his arm. Blood scented the water, further agitating my sharks. Bright light flashed and a killer whale appeared where Kupua had been treading water. The orca flicked its fin and charged the blue who gave way to the larger predator. Kupua swerved toward Nikko and I, whooshing past us toward the swirling vortex of churning water. We stalked after him until the powerful maelstrom wrenched us all from our path and into its grip. Nikko flipped and rolled in the turmoil and I tumbled off his back. My vision blurred as I spun over and over, caught in the vortex being sucked downward. As the current flung me around I glimpsed Nikko several feet below being tossed round and round like a coin dropped into a funnel. His panic wrenched through my soul.

A long shadow darkened the water from above as a thirty-foot wooden sailing ship was sucked into the black hole, careening toward me. Before I could twist in the current and avoid the oncoming collision, the orca rammed the hull and shifted the boat a fraction from my head. Bubbles whooshed in my ear and a crack thundered through the water. Both ship and whale plunged deeper into the maelstrom. Shards and splinters torpedoed through the current like bullets shot from a rifle and one jammed into my arm with a jolt of pain. Wincing, I yanked it out and tumbled in the ships' wake, hoping to catch a glimpse of my brother. Concern flickered like a spark across my thoughts. Kupua had just risked his life for me. Why?

I couldn't sense Nikko nearby and my legs shook from the energy it took trying to kick free from the grip of the whirlpool. Frustration, worry and regret warred in my heart.

Tightening my hold on the spear, I heaved it over my head and ignited its power. Vibration shivered down my arm and I twisted slightly against the current. Immediately, the sea calmed and I ceased my descent into darkness. Nikko shot up from the blackness below and rubbed against my arm as I exhaled in relief.

A quick scan of the area failed to reveal my brother's location. Where could be be? Or maybe better, what form had he taken? I shouted to the depths, "Keep your promise! Bring me to Eka!"

An orca appeared beneath me, its camouflaged dark back making it almost impossible to spot until it was within a few feet. With a flash of bright light, my brother's eyes stared into mine, a tinge of sadness flitting across his expression. Regret tugged at my heart for a moment before frustration surged. "Where is Eka?"

"She's in your home, safe and watched over by Tessa. I told you, we would never place her in danger."

I swung onto Nikko's back, anxious to check on her.

"Wait," My brother called. "She is close to delivery and will need medical care. This is her first baby. Please consider allowing Kele to help with the birth. Call a truce to our differences for her sake."

My chest tightened. "I'll not allow any harm to come to her. It is not your concern." My shoulders relaxed and I remembered what he'd done for me and sighed. "Thank you for what you did with that ship, I won't forget it. But Eka is not your responsibility. I will take care of her."

"Family is always my concern, brother."

"You stopped being family a long time ago." Wrapping my arms around Nikko's thick torso, we charged toward Seamount, leaving Kupua in our wake. A small ache, one I'd not felt since being a boy, grew with the distance between us.

CHAPTER 18

TESSA

'EHA

PAIN

"Eka, sit down and rest, Moho will be back soon."

Eka arched with one hand around her bulging stomach and the other rubbing her lower back. "I can't get comfortable. Does it seem hot in here to you?"

"No." I strode over to where she paced and felt her forehead. "You're burning up. This isn't good, Eka. We should have Kele check you out."

Her forehead creased with worry. "I'm not going anywhere until I talk to Moho." Her round doe eyes softened. "You should go before he gets home, I don't think I can handle anymore conflict right now. I appreciate the picnic and everything you've done, but you know Moho won't be happy to find you here." She paced, shaking her head. "I'm worried. He's been gone too long."

Guilt tightened my throat. "I have a confession, Eka. I did want to see you but there's more to my visit."

She stilled and narrowed her eyes at me. "What do you mean?"

"Moho created a whirlpool with his weather spear and it threatened our sea as well as surface dwellers. Fish, turtles and coral were dying. We had to stop it. Please understand. So many lives were at stake." I cleared my throat. "So Kupua and I lured him to the site by saying we'd taken you there, but only to force him to put an end to it. We meant no harm to him, but we had to protect our ocean. I'm sorry I didn't tell you this up front but I didn't want to upset you. I'm so sorry."

Her fists clenched at her side and she closed her eyes, speaking softly. "I trusted you, Queen Tessa. If Moho comes to any harm…I don't know what I'll do. I can't raise a child alone. Do you even care about him?" She opened her eyes and tears spilled onto her cheeks.

I wrapped my arms around her shoulders and hugged her tight. "Yes, we care very much. Kupua won't let anything happen to Moho. He'll be back soon. If there were trouble I would know it. And, you'll never be alone sweetie. There are so many people who love you, including me."

She pushed away from me. "Moho may not be perfect, but there is love in his heart, because I've felt it." Her eyes gleamed as they met mine. "He's changing." She rubbed her belly fondly, whispering, "This baby is helping him find himself again. Even the Lua Pele can't compete with our child."

"I hope you're right." Maybe Eka had a point and her baby was the key to reaching Moho. A voice in my head caught my attention. *Moho's on his way home. Time to leave, Ipo."*

"Eka, Moho will be home soon. Kupua just told me he is safe and on his way. It's time for me to leave."

She nodded and reached out her hand before suddenly doubling over with a scream. “Ahhhhh.” Her knees buckled and I caught her and eased her onto her bed in the corner.

“What’s wrong?”

“I don’t know,” she panted, “it’s too soon for the baby to come.”

“Tell me what you’re feeling. Where does it hurt?”

She pointed to her side. “Sharp pain in my side.” Muscles in her face clenched and she let out a groan. “I need Moho.”

“He’ll be here soon but we need to get you medical care. Please, let me call Kele. If not for you, then for your baby’s sake.”

A growl from the doorway sent a shiver down my spine. “Get away from her, Tessa. What have you done?”

I pivoted on my heels and stepped away from Eka to face Moho. “Something is wrong and she needs help. Let me call Kele. He’ll know what to do.”

He strode to her side and kneeled next to the bed, clasping her hand in his own. “Eka, are you okay?”

“I’m not sure.” She tucked his hand beneath her cheek. “It hurts, Moho.”

With his free hand, Moho gently caressed her stomach. “You need to stay in bed. No more doing anything. I’ll take care of you and our baby.”

She nodded, before releasing another groan and clutching her stomach. Sweat broke out on her brow. Moho glanced over his shoulder at me. “Leave, Tessa. I don’t want you here for the birth.”

"The pain isn't supposed to be sharp. Her temperature is too high. I don't think this is labor, Moho. Please let me get Kele. I promise you we only want to do what is best for Eka and the baby. We mean no harm. Let us help you."

Eka stroked his arm. "Maybe she's right. Please, I don't want to risk our child."

Moho's chest fell in a sigh. "We can't trust them."

She kissed his hand. "Tessa has never hurt me and I believe she truly cares about what happens to our child."

He glared over his shoulder at me. "Fine. Call Kele. But only him. Kupua is not to come with him."

"Got it." I sent the message to Kupua who lingered close by, waiting for me, urging him to hurry. "I'll wait for him near the entrance. Kele will be here soon, Eka." I spun on my heels and ran to wait for Kele.

Sid met me at the entrance, letting me know Kele wasn't far behind. "Kupua can't enter, so reassure him I'm fine. As soon as we know if Eka's okay, I'll head home."

Sid wrapped a tentacle around my ankle and squeezed, his suction cups pulsating against my skin. Squatting to get closer, I ran my fingers across his slick body. "I love you too, you crazy octopus."

Releasing his grip, Sid slipped into the water, and minutes later, Kele emerged. Water streamed off him as he scrambled through the entrance with his pack in hand, smelling of garlic and mint. His big grin relaxed the knot building in my stomach. "You one hardcore sistah tinking you can help da brah, Moho. Dey call you nochanic on da surface. Dat means a sistah who tinks she can do something she cannot."

"Never give up, Kele, that's my motto."

"Dat fo'sure. Show me da way to Eka and I see wat I can do."

As we approached Eka's room, Moho's voice rumbled down the hall. "You're too trusting, Eka. If Kele hurts you, I'll have no choice but to tear him apart."

Kele tensed next to me for a split second before shaking his head and arms as if to remind himself of his mission. He strode with confidence into the room. "Moho, my brah, I no skeda-u. You make any trouble and I going to smood you."

The air crackled with tension reminding me of storms on the mainland right before lightning struck. Moho's fists clenched and a growl vibrated his chest. "Give me your word you won't hurt her."

"Broddah, we family. You may be lolo but I am a healer. I'm here to help you."

With a slight nod, Moho backed up a step and motioned for Kele to get closer to Eka. Kele's keen eyes assessed her and he quickly kneeled and opened his pack. "Tell me wat ya feeling."

Eka explained her pain as Kele gently prodded her swollen body. Her face scrunched in a grimace when he touched her abdomen. "Any other symptoms da last few days?"

"I've had headaches lately, but nothing else."

Kele swiveled on his heels and looked straight at Moho. "Dis little wahine needs to stay in bed. Dis can be serious and she needs to be near da healing pool at Moku-ola. Garans she need help wit the delivery."

"What's wrong with her?"

He twisted around to look at Eka and took her hand in his. "On da surface dey call dis preclampsia. It means you have to rest or it could be bad fo' you and da baby." He glanced over his shoulder at Moho. "I no bulai you. Dis brutal. Let us take her to Moku-ola."

Moho paced the length of the room, his eyes on the floor. "You can treat her here. This is her home and the safest place for her and the baby."

"You lolo, brah. Dis not safe fo' her."

Eka twisted on the bed and screamed in agony. Kele whipped out several packets and tossed them to me. "Hurry. Get da water boiling and mix dis in it." I scrambled to the corner and whipped out one of Kele's fire stones and dumped the contents of the packet into a pan with some water. As it heated, garlic vapors swirled into the air.

Kele stood and faced off with Moho, his hands clenched at his side. "Fo' real brah, I nevah lie to you. If you care fo' her, let us move her to Moku-ola."

Moho stood motionless, his eyes flicking between Kele and Eka. "I need your word and Tessa's that you will heal her and allow us to leave unharmed when she is able. A truce agreement between us or she stays here."

Kele spun and gave me a nod. "Queen Tessa, dat is your agreement fo' make."

"Kupua and I have always wanted peace with you and I agree to a truce and hope it will be more someday, Moho. We love Eka and will do everything we can to help her and the baby. So yes, we are in agreement."

He grunted and motioned to Kele. "So how do we get her there safely?"

His slight bristled my nerves, but I spoke calmly, not giving Kele a chance to speak. "We have a submarine that will take her there, bed and all. She won't have to move."

"Good." Moho knelt next to Eka and held her hand. She rested her cheek against his fingers.

While Kele finished brewing the garlic and kelp tea for Eka, I called for Kupua to have Akalei bring the submarine. "The sub is on the way. They should be here in a few minutes."

Kele held up a cup to Eka. "Drink dis. It help wit da pain."

She scooted up on the bed and cradled the cup in her hands. "Thank you, Kele." She locked eyes with Moho over the rim as she sipped. She loved him. I sent a silent prayer to the Creator that she and the baby would be okay.

I quietly stepped next to Kele as he packed up the remains of his supplies and searched his eyes for clues to how much hope he carried about the situation. He laid his hand on my shoulder and determination settled over his features. He wasn't about to give up. A sigh of relief escaped my lips and I leaned my head on his thick arm.

Not long after Eka finished her tea, Akalei arrived with the submarine. She strode up to Moho and Eka with the confidence of someone who refused to see anything but the best in others. She leaned over and planted a kiss on Eka's cheek. "Hey, sweetie, we've got the sub all ready for you. Your family sends their love and can't wait to see you."

Moho shifted uneasily, his voice rough. "All visitors will come through me. Eka isn't staying long. This is her home and once she is healed, she'll be coming back here. Don't forget that."

Akalei turned on him with both hands on her hips. "It's not a competition. There's enough love to go around, Moho. You remember that."

Before he could reply, Akalei stalked out of the room and down the hall. I sighed. "Enough talking. Moho, pick up one end of the bed. Kele, you grab the other. It's time to get Eka moved."

CHAPTER 19

TESSA

KAUHALE

HOME

Silence cloaked the entrance when we arrived. On my orders, everyone had stayed away. We didn't need a scene. The tea had done its work and Eka slept during the journey and didn't stir much as Moho and Kele transported her bed from the sub down the cavernous path to our home. Soft green light cast from the bioluminescent rocks, spun shadows at my feet as I lead our group. Thoughts swirled around my head as I struggled to grasp how to convince Moho we meant him no harm. With the massive door in front of me, an idea struck. I lifted my hand to touch the intricate carvings and glanced over my shoulder. "Moho, this is your home. The door will recognize you, just as it does me. Help me unlock it."

His body stilled as my words hung in the air. I swallowed, sending a silent prayer to the Creator that I hadn't made a mistake. Without speaking, he and Kele lowered Eka's bed onto the sandy gravel. Moho stalked to the door and stood next to me, his head high but avoiding any eye contact. He placed his hand next to mine and the door creaked and groaned, opening into a brightly lit entryway paved in abalone shell.

Next to me, Moho released his breath, as if he'd been unsure if the door would accept his request for entry. Peace settled over my heart.

"We're home, Moho."

Without a word, he spun on his heel and returned to lift Eka's bed. We quietly marched through the house and down the stairs until we reached the healing room. Thick, warm, humidity wrapped around us as I cracked open the door and stood aside so Eka could be carried inside. Kelp hung from the ceiling on drying racks and a tinge of mint spiced the air.

"Set her down near da pool," Kele instructed. Once the bed was settled, Moho sat on the floor next to Eka's head, his legs crossed and hands in his lap. Moisture mingled with sweat, glistening on his caramel colored skin. I'd never seen him wear a shirt beneath the sea. The mark of his gift, circular symbols surrounding a shark, a tattoo he was born with, shimmered on his thick chest. Heavy ropes of muscles twitched along his arms. "Leave us alone."

Kele stood over him, a stubborn look plastered on his face. "Fo' now, brah. But I will check on her soon. You go make trouble all you want, ainokea. I da doctor and will take care fo' her." Without waiting for Moho's response, he stormed out and I followed.

"Nice job," I whispered to him outside the door.

He winked. "He acking all tuff but he no make beef wit me. Not wen she needs me."

"You take care of them, I'm going to find Kupua." I stretched on my tip-toes and kissed his cheek. "You're the best, Kele."

He tucked his head against his shoulder in a shrug. "Awww…tank you."

Kupua wasn't hard to locate. He lingered in the hall just outside the healing room. A frown creased his brow and he tugged me into his arms. "I missed you."

Snuggling against his chest, I whispered, "I missed you too."

"How is Eka?"

"I'm not sure. Right now she's resting."

"Kele will take good care of her. You hungry?"

"Famished."

"Let's grab some food and put together something to bring back for our guests."

Halfway to the kitchen, we collided with Loli, Eka's mom. Dark circles framed her eyes and she wrung her hands as she spoke. "I'm on my way to see Eka. How is she?"

"She's resting right now and Kele is taking care of her. He doesn't want the baby to come too early and will keep a close eye on her."

She took a step around me but I grabbed her arm. "Moho is right by her side and very protective. Be careful."

Her shoulders stiffened. "If he's going to be part of our family, then he will have to get used to all of us. He's not the only one who cares about her."

I released my grip and smiled at her. "She's lucky to have you, Loli."

She returned my smile and hustled past to get to the healing room.

Kupua squeezed my shoulder. "You miss your mom."

"Yeah. But I'm pretty lucky to have you, Rachel, and all our friends, so no complaining here."

He spun me to face him and wiped a tear from trailing down my cheek. "It's okay to grieve. It doesn't mean you're not grateful for what you have, just remembering what you've lost."

Warmth curled around my heart. "You always know just what to say."

He winked. "That's my job." We held hands the rest of the way to the kitchen.

A hot, steamy, pot of vegetable stew greeted us, flooding the air with warmth and spice. We each filled a bowl and wandered out to eat while looking over the city. The pathways below were empty, with most people tucked into their homes for the night. Torches flickered, casting shadows across the calm water of the sacred pool. Overhead the ocean swirled and I could see shapes floating just outside the clear ceiling. While our city lay tucked within lava stone, the ceiling was carved from pure quartz and totally transparent. A true window to the sea. A sigh escaped me as I licked my spoon clean of stew. "Is it possible Moho's heart might really be healing?"

"I believe anything is possible with the Creators' love. He's definitely fighting an internal battle. Maybe this child will be the tipping point."

Before I could respond, Akalei shouted behind us. "Tessa, Kupua, hurry, Kele needs you. Moho's gone bezerk."

CHAPTER 20

MOHO

PIO

CAPTIVE

As Eka slumbered next to me in the healing room, black fog inched along the periphery of my vision. Tendrils reached for me and each touch of the dark mist lanced my skin with searing pain like being stabbed with a firecracker. A voice scraped across my mind. *Return home now. You are mine and cannot stay here. These are your enemies. Do not defy me.* The Lua Pele had found me.

My heartbeat quickened, pounding as if it would burst from my chest. Pain was a familiar companion, so I inhaled deeply and absorbed it while clearing my mind of all distractions. A new voice emerged from the depth of my soul, warm and soft, it drifted into my mind like a comforting breeze. *You are loved, my son, and always welcome here. This is where you were created to live. Be at peace here.* My heart slowed and relaxed into the warmth of this embrace like a starved child receiving a meal. Could it be true?

Fire erupted along my spine with enough force to smash my face into the floor. *Lies. Betrayal. Do you not remember?*

Images of my youth flashed in front of my eyes. Sharks responding to my anger, attacking my friends while I watched. I couldn't stop them, didn't understand yet my power. The day my gift had activated was the worst of my life. The Lua Pele had offered help, shown me how to conquer my new skill. Confusion tangled all my thoughts together in a jumble of knots. Synapses in my brain sparked like fishing barbs digging into my head. Agony clouded my mind and I lashed out, colliding against chairs and tables, tossing them out of my way. A roar built in my chest and I released it, oblivious to anything but the internal battle I fought. *Yes. Show them who you are. Destroy them and take your place as king.*

Rising to my feet, I flung my arms into the air and crashed against the hanging racks. Latching onto the metal, I ripped one from the ceiling and heaved it against the far wall, sending pieces of kelp, cloth and dried spices flying in all directions. "Stop!" I shouted to the voices in my head as I whipped from right to left in search of something to demolish.

"Ka-moho-ali, it's okay. Moho, my son, listen to my voice." My head swiveled toward the soft voice. A tall silhouette in the doorway caught my eye. Focusing took all my effort, but slowly a face emerged from the cloud of blurry shapes.

"Mother?"

"Yes, It's me. It's going to be okay. Focus on my voice." Hiiakka slid closer, one hand extended.

"Don't touch me." I edged backward. As my vision cleared, other faces came into view behind her. Kele, my brother, Tessa, and a smaller woman I didn't recognize. Clarity slowly returned and I spun to check Eka who was awake on the bed, her eyes wide with fear. Shame slammed into me and I staggered against the wall, no longer able to sustain my own weight.

"Moho, take my hand. It will be okay."

"No, it's not okay. You can't help me. Nobody can help me."

Her soft voice didn't waiver. "That's a lie, son. Don't believe it. Take my hand and come with me to the healing pool."

"Why? Since when do you care?"

Tears welled in her eyes but she continued to inch forward. "I've always cared about you. Your family has never stopped loving you. Let me show you. Please, just give us a chance."

"You weren't there when I needed you. Why should things be different now?"

"I'm sorry I wasn't there when you discovered your gift. It came to you earlier than we expected. If we had known, your father and I would never have let you travel to the open ocean without us. Please forgive us. Come with me to the healing pool, it will help."

Her words sunk into my heart bringing a soothing calm I hadn't expected. "Fine. I'll follow you to the pool." I refused her hand but trudged after her to the healing pool. Vapors of steam rose from the water's surface, cloaking the pool in a veil of warm, white fog. Hot water welcomed me and swirled around my stiff and sore muscles, soothing those spots where I'd been stung by pain. Lavender and chamomile calmed my senses and cleared my mind. Bubbles rose above my head as I descended to the bottom. My mother settled across from me, fully submerging into the 20 foot depth of the pool. Sand covered the bottom and provided a soft cushion for us both. No whispers haunted me as the warmth wrapped me in its embrace. With a clear head I lifted my chin and looked into my mother's gentle eyes. "The

Lua Pele will never let me go. I cannot stay in this place. Once the baby is born, Eka and I will return to Seamount. This is no longer my home."

"No Ka-Moho-ali, you are wrong. This is where you belong. You are a prince of Moku-ola. The Creator is stronger than the evil that poisons you. We can all help you break free."

She used my formal name. It rolled off her tongue with familiarity that comforted some long lost part of me. "And then what? I skulk around the city like some second-class loser? I am a king and will never be a follower."

"You are a member of the royal family. Join Kupua and Tessa in leading our people. If you work together, nothing will threaten our people or the ocean we protect. That is what you were born to be."

Emotions stirred in my heart as bitter words teetered on my tongue, but before I could utter them a rush of warmth surged around me, soaking me in wave of overwhelming love. *She loves you, Moho. Do not speak out of pride or bitterness. Forgive her.*

As if she'd heard the Creator's words, my mother spoke. "Will you ever forgive me, Ka-Moho-ali? Will you ever accept my love for you?"

The fleeting peace I'd felt in the pool vanished and I shoved my feet against the sand and popped to the surface. "It's not that easy mother." Part of me yearned to rid myself of the bitterness I'd nurtured for so long, but another part gripped my heart like a vise, unable to relinquish my hurt. "I need some time alone." My skin shivered at the loss of warmth as I emerged from the water and stalked from the room, dripping a trail of salty droplets behind me. Keeping my gaze forward, I marched out of the healing rooms and down the hall until I found a secluded corner to sink into. I pushed my back against the wall, and slid to a crouch, covering my face with my hands. The lingering smell of lavender on my fingers provided some measure of comfort. Why was I so confused? For years the only voice I'd heard was the Lua Pele. Where had the Creator been when I'd been scared and alone in the darkness of the ocean caves I'd fled to during my transition? My mother's voice filled my thoughts. Could her words be true? Did she truly regret not being there for me? Questions and doubts burrowed under my skin, challenging all the truths I'd been so sure of for the past few years.

Eka's scream shattered my solitude and I jerked up and rushed back to the healing room to find Kele at her side. His voice was heavy with worry. "It's not da baby. She's gone lolo."

CHAPTER 21

MOHO

HOA PAIO

ENEMY

Eka huddled in a corner of the bed with her hands crossed over her chest. Her face contorted in pain. "Help, Moho. It has me."

I brushed Kele aside and leaned over her. Her skin shone with a sickly shade of blue and her breathing labored as if she couldn't get enough oxygen. A strong odor of rotten eggs surrounded her and terror lit her eyes. "What is wrong, Eka? What has you?"

She coughed and gagged, her shoulders shaking and chest heaving. "The Lua Pele. It's choking me. Can't you see it? Get it off of me."

Every muscle tensed as dread stabbed it's talons into my heart. The Lua Pele had always attacked me, never those around me. "I can't see it. It's not attacking you in physical form. This is a mind game. You have to fight it Eka."

"It's too strong. I can't get enough air."

I clutched her arms. "No. You can do this. You are my queen and carry our child. Fight for our child. Don't give up."

She flung her head back and forth and grappled with an unseen force around her throat. Tessa pushed between Kele and I and touched Eka's arm. "Eka, ask for the Creator's help. Invite him into your heart. He can stop this. He is stronger than this evil."

A growl rumbled from my chest. "Stay out of this, Tessa. You do not know what you're dealing with."

She scowled at me. "Yes, I do. You left me in the Lua Pele's lair, remember? It was the Creator who rescued me and he can do the same for Eka. Do you have a better idea?"

"No." I released my grip on Eka. The memory of leaving her in the Lua Pele's lair flooded my thoughts. I'd never known exactly how she had escaped. The first person to ever to be freed from the depths of that cavern. At the time it had enraged me, but now, a seed of gratefulness sparked.

Tessa grasped Eka's hands and asked, "Eka, nod your head if you are ready to give yourself into the care of the Creator and seek his help."

Eka's eyes frantically searched mine and the terror reflected in their depths chilled my bones. I nodded to her and she flicked her gaze to Tessa and bobbed her head in agreement.

"Good. Then on your behalf, I declare the Creator victor in this battle and thank him for his protection. He promises that he will never leave us and will always protect us. There is no force in the world more powerful. So, in the name of our Creator, I command the Lua Pele to release you right now!"

No. A voice hissed over our heads. *She is mine.*

Tessa leaned closer to Eka and tightened her grip on Eka's hands. "Eka, can you say you agree. That you choose to belong to the Creator?"

Muscles in Eka's face and neck strained. A raspy whisper escaped her lips. "I agree."

Tessa raised her voice. "This woman belongs to the Creator. Lua Pele, you must release her. She is not yours!"

A sweet fragrance drowned out the foul smell of evil, like a fresh breeze on a hot day. The shaking eased and Eka gulped in air, gasping and choking as her airways cleared. Color returned to her cheeks and the blue tint around her lips faded. Kele squeezed between Tessa and I to examine her and I exhaled in relief. Tessa ducked behind me and turned to leave but I snatched her arm. "Thank you."

"No need to thank me. It was the Creator who saved her." She leveled her eyes at me. "He can save you as well."

"It was your faith. The Lua Pele has never attacked like this before. It is not me I am worried about. I need to destroy it before the baby arrives or my child will be its next target."

"How?"

"It's better you don't know. Just promise to take care of Eka for me."

Kupua captured my wrist and wrenched it from Tessa's arm. "Keep your hands off her."

We faced each other, chest to chest and I could almost taste his fear for Tessa. "I wasn't going to harm her, I was thanking her. I'm leaving."

"Wait." Tessa inserted herself between us. "Kupua, he's planning on destroying the Lua Pele. We have to help him."

My brother's face paled. "The Lua Pele can't be destroyed, not even by you, Moho. You should know that better than anyone."

I jerked past him. "I didn't ask for your help. Just take care of Eka."

"Wait. How do you plan on doing this?"

I clenched my fists and grumbled. "You don't need to concern yourself. I'll take care of it."

"He thinks the Lua Pele will destroy Eka and the baby if he doesn't do something," Tessa pleaded with Kupua.

"Brother, if you are determined to go after this thing, let us help you. If you really want to protect Eka and the baby, then don't be stupid. Getting yourself killed won't help them. They need you alive. The more people in this battle, the better your chance of success…and it will be a battle."

His words made sense. It had been a long time since I'd had anyone but my sharks to fight by my side. "Fine. But there's something I need to do before we leave. Something to ensure that if I don't return, my child will receive the honor he or she deserves as royalty."

Kupua narrowed his eyes. "What might that be?"

"I need to marry Eka."

CHAPTER 22

TESSA

PU'IWA

SURPRISE

“Shouldn’t you ask her first?” I flinched as Moho clenched his fists and the muscle in his jaw pulsed. Without speaking, he marched back into the healing room and next to Eka’s bed.

“Everyone out, except the healer and Tessa.”

Kupua clasped his mother’s hand and led her out, along with Akalei and Eka’s mom, their footsteps a distant echo against the now silent walls of the room. Moho lowered to one knee and cradled Eka’s hand in his.

“What’s wrong Moho? Why did you send everyone away?”

“Eka, it is my job to keep you and our child safe. Do you trust me?”

She leaned across the bed and planted a kiss on his cheek. “You know I do.”

His gentleness shocked me. This was a side of Moho I’d never seen. Even his voice flowed like a caress. "Good. The Lua Pele must be destroyed before the baby arrives, but before I do this I want to ensure your future. Tessa is going to marry us, right now, so if I don't return, my son or daughter will be recognized as part of the royal family."

Tears welled in Eka's eyes and her lower lip trembled. "I want to marry you, but because you love me, not to fulfill some duty." She rubbed her hand over her swollen belly. "We don't need your pity."

"This isn't pity. We are a family now. I love you and our child, Eka. There has never been another. You know this is true, so don't make me beg."

She cupped his face with her hand. "Yes. I'll marry you."

He shifted his gaze to me. "Do it now. Kele can bear witness."

My mouth felt like cotton balls had taken up residence. This was happening so fast. "I've never officiated a wedding before."

"It doesn't matter. As queen, you are the only one who can do it. Say the words."

I glanced over at Eka. "Are you sure? Is this really what you want?"

She smiled and shook her head furiously. "Absolutely. Moho is right, we are already family."

I spread my hands before me and bowed my head. "Creator, this couple, Ka-Moho-ali and Eka, come before you to say vows and join as husband and wife. I ask for your blessing on this union." I nodded at Moho. "Speak your vows."

"I take you as my wife, Eka, to protect and to honor. I give my life as a shield for you and our child. I pledge my love and loyalty to you for as long as I live."

Eka's face blazed with joy and her voice cracked as she spoke. "I take you as my husband, Ka-Moho-ali, to cherish and love. I promise my loyalty and heart to you."

My eyes caught Kele's. "Kele do you stand as witness to these vows?"

Kele cleared his throat. "I bear witness fo dis union, to da promises dey make and da vows made."

Moho and Eka held each other's gaze as if they would devour one another as I spoke. "Then with the authority given to me by the Creator, as your queen, I declare your vows accepted and your marriage witnessed and sealed. You are husband and wife."

Moho wrapped his hand around the back of Eka's head and kissed her. She moaned slightly and sunk into his embrace. Kele coughed and turned to leave but Moho tore himself from Eka and stopped him. "Stay. I have to leave. Take care of her." He stroked Eka's face in a rare show of tenderness. "This is to secure the safety of you and our child. It is the only reason I would leave your side right now. I'll return as quickly as I can."

Eka clutched his hand and kissed his palm. "Don't go. I need you here, Moho. Please. Stay. We can figure out how to get rid of this Lua Pele after the baby is born."

He peeled her hand from his flesh and stood. "This is not a discussion." He stalked from the room and I followed, recognizing he hadn't changed that much. Baby steps.

He swept past Kupua who waited outside the door and continued plowing down the hall and up the stairs. We chased after him, hopping two steps at a time to keep up.

"So, what's your plan?"

"No plan."

"Okay. Don't you think we need one?"

"Plan all you want. I'm getting the spear and taking out its lair."

Kupua shot me a worried look. "You can't use the spear, it's too dangerous."

Moho paused and scowled over his shoulder. "Dangerous is exactly what I need to destroy such a creature."

"Yeah, but you haven't had the best luck controlling the spear's impact and may take out more than just the Lua Pele." I chimed in, ignoring the hostility oozing from his every pore.

"If you're scared, don't come, just stay out of my way." He dismissed me and leapt off the last stair and rumbled into the hall. Irked, I chased after him.

"Hey, I'm not scared, just practical. It's not in my best interest to end up with you dead and the Lua Pele angry for revenge. Not in Eka's best interest either."

He grunted and kept jogging until we all skidded to a stop at the waters edge. The small lagoon entrance to my home now crammed with thrashing sharks. Water sprayed the air as they whipped their fins in agitation. Moho sneered at Kupua and I. "Still ready to join my team?"

Kupua snorted and dove into the crowded fray, morphing into an orca as he crashed into the water and made his own splash.

CHAPTER 23

TESSA

LOKO 'INO

EVIL

Kupua and I trudged after Moho as he marched into the soul room of his home in Seamount, his back straight and head high. Muscles in his back clenched and twitched, giving a clue to the anxiety he battled. Kupua twined his fingers with mine and I leaned against his shoulder as we walked, soaking in his strength and love. He bent over and whispered into my ear. "The Creator is with us and he is more powerful than the Lua Pele. We can do this."

The knot in my chest loosened like a flower blooming in the blaze of the sun. I squeezed his hand in agreement. We could face this together. Ahead, vapors of steam circled Moho's feet as if they were tendrils of a living monster spreading across the floor. Sulfur burned my nose and sweat sheened my skin as the temperature spiked. Sparks shot from the fissure near his throne where the spear rested.

"It knows we're here," Moho said as he leapt over the crack and landed on his throne, sweeping up the spear and swiveling to face us. Grim determination hardened his features and Kupua and I stopped in our tracks. "It does not yet know our intent."

Flames erupted from the floor and created a barrier between Moho and us. We were completely cut off. Blasts of scorching steam forced Kupua and I to retreat toward the entrance. Heat flushed my face. I shouted across the divide. "Use the spear!"

"It will destroy my home if I attack here. I can't lose Seamount." As if on cue, the flames licked higher until we could no longer glimpse Moho through their red haze, but heard him groan in pain.

Kupua inched closer to the wall of blazing red heat. "You have no choice, brother. You must fight and shut down this stronghold."

Shafts of blue and green flared through the steaming haze with a vibrating hum, which sounded a little like a chainsaw slicing through logs. Brilliant colors surrounded the flames, dousing them like water on a fire. Moho jammed the spear into the fissure, sweat dripping from his face with the exertion. His flesh ripped open across his arms and chest, ragged and swollen with blood oozing onto the rocks surrounding the crack. As the fissure swallowed the flames, a low rumble rocked the floor underneath our feet.

Kupua grabbed my arm and yanked me backwards. "We have to get out of here, the place is going to crumble." His voice raised above the chaos. "Enough. Time to leave, brother. Now."

Moho met our gaze, his eyes glazed with anguish that slowly cleared as Kupua's words sunk in. He nodded and yanked the spear from within the widening gap and vaulted across the yawning divide, landing with a thud in front of us. The spear glistened with power, blue and green swirling within its shaft. A brilliant jewel on the hilt lit like a lightbulb. Moho stroked his thumb across the jewel and the colors faded and the spear quieted as he tucked it under his arm.

Boulders of volcanic rock crashed around us as the ceiling broke apart. We bolted towards the sea, racing through the halls as walls of rocks tumbled on both sides. With a groan, our path shook and quickly disintegrated into the sea. Waves exploded through the sand and gravel, and sucked us into a swirling vortex of debris. Blackness engulfed my vision and the water clouded with silt, dust and rock, creating a zero visibility environment. I tried to kick free of the rubble but my foot caught in a tangle of the mess and held me in place. Using my hands to locate what held me captive, I curled into a ball and tugged at a mesh of net and sludge wrapped around my foot. A large boulder collided with my shoulder and sent a crack of pain shuddering through my back. My chest tightened and I fought the panic rolling through me. An arm wrapped around my waist and jerked me free before flinging me onto the back of a shark. My arms and legs clung to the beast and I whispered my thanks into its mind. We torpedoed toward the surface, dodging a barrage of floating debris. An orca swam to our side and rubbed its sleek back against my leg.

The shark left me at the surface and Kupua changed back into human form. We swam in a circle, shocked at what we found. The entire island of Seamount was decimated, submerged beneath the ocean swells. All that remained were bits of wood and furniture bobbing in the waves. It was as if a giant vacuum had sucked it into a black hole.

I slung my arm over Kupua's shoulder and buried my face in his neck. "Thank you for freeing me, I was starting to panic."

He raised an eyebrow at me. "You were stuck? It wasn't me who freed you. Are you hurt?" He ran his hands over my shoulder and arms, examining me closely.

"Just bruised I think, nothing broken. I'll be sore for awhile."

Moho's head popped up next to us, a large gash above his eye swelled the side of his face. "That went well."

I clutched his arm and planted a wet kiss on his cheek. "You helped me. Thank you."

He shoved me away and growled. "I'm not your friend. Eka and I need you right now but nothing else has changed."

"You're wrong. You have changed, you just won't admit it."

He scowled and lifted the spear above the water. "We're not finished with this battle. Are you ready to fight, or do you want to hang here and chat me up?"

"You're such a charmer. We're with you. Lead the way." I said and dove beneath the surface, grabbing onto Kupua's dorsal fin after he changed into an orca. My back and shoulder were stiff but not enough to stop me from ending this war. We followed Moho into the chilly depths, heading far from the warmth of our home waters. He rode Nikko whose slate blue skin and subtle, faded stripes, blended so well he almost disappeared into the gray murky sea. Moho molded perfectly to Nikko's back, creating the image of a seamless creature, gliding through the currents in an effortless dance of agility and grace.

I stroked Kupua's sleek side and pressed my cheek against his back. "Your brother is coming around."

His hope burned across my mind like a flash of white lightning. We held that hope between us as a shield against the dread threading the barren waters we approached. Four tiger sharks flanked our sides, mouths slightly open to reveal rows of razor sharp teeth. A quick search of their minds revealed Moho commanded them to guard our descent into the Lua Pele's domain. Gray inked to black as we dove farther from the bright surface and my wristbands ignited to light our way. The soft green glow pierced the veil of darkness with a halo of light. A shiver ran through me, a mixture of anticipation and memory of my last visit to this place. Moho had brought me here as a prisoner not so long ago but the Creator had freed me. Now I prayed my brother–in-law would experience a similar freedom. Nerves tingled along my skin and I clung tighter to Kupua for comfort.

The sea floor lay barren beneath our feet as we stood before the lava cave entrance to the Lua Pele's lair. Kupua morphed into human form and clasped my hand in his own. His warmth pulsed through my skin with a soothing caress. Moho's sharks patrolled in circles above our heads like the quiet but lethal guardians they were. This close to the lair, the water nearly simmered with heat. Columns of bubbles shot from random places in the sea floor in tiny explosions of fury. Boulders of lava rocks glimmered with red from within, casting eerie shadows against Moho and Kupua's face. A tinge of sulfur clouded the ocean, sickening my stomach. Moho nodded and took a step toward the entrance, but before he set his foot into the silt, a violent shaking rocked the ground. Blasts of putrid air sprayed from the opening, gagging us with the smell of rotten flesh and death. We clutched at each other's arms to gain balance and strength.

As one, we forged through the stench and pressurized heat to pass beneath the crumbling rock and into the lair. Once inside, stale air replaced heated ocean and we released our grips on one another. "It knows we're here," Moho grumbled. The muscles on his chest and arms tensed. Red welts still peppered his skin from our last encounter with the Lua Pele.

"Then let's not waste time." Kupua answered and pointed at the spear gripped in Moho's palm.

"Not here, I've got to get deeper in. You don't need to go any farther. Wait for me."

I shook my head. "No. We stay together. If you're going, so are we. It will take the strength of all of us with our Creator to win this victory. Lead the way."

A flicker of surprise crossed his face before being replaced with resolve. He jogged into the hazy red glow of the cave's interior. Kupua and I followed, our feet splatting in the green sludge coating the floor. I groaned as thick grime oozed between my toes. Something slithered to my left and I shuddered, forcing my eyes on the path ahead. Seaweed dangled from the ceiling like slimy arms reaching for us. A heavy oppression settled on our shoulders like a thick blanket on a hot day. Heat intensified with every step deeper into the lair and threatened to suffocate us with its potency.

Whispers of lies threaded my thoughts. *You are returned. You are not strong enough to defeat me. You will be mine.*

My steps faltered and Kupua's arms steadied me. "Keep your thoughts focused on the Creator. Do not acknowledge the lies."

I nodded, grateful for his encouragement. Ahead, Moho stumbled and moaned. As I reached for his arm, I gasped. Angry red welts burst across his skin as if he'd been whipped with a stick. "Do not touch me." His eyes burned with pain and fury like the molten lava glowing from within the rock walls. Sweat beaded his forehead. Without the rocks to insulate the heat, it would be too much to bear.

"Brother, you knew this would not be easy. We need to hurry, before more damage is done."

His lips pressed together in a grim line of determination as he lifted the spear firmly gripped in his hand. Lines burrowed in his face, hinting at what it cost him to push forward.

We turned down a dark, steamy corridor, lit dimly by the pulsing red of the rock. Black mist swirled around our feet, spearing dread into our pores where it brushed our flesh. "Hurry," I urged, battling the despondency pricking my thoughts. Kupua leaned close and snatched my hand, linking his strength to mine as we jogged after Moho.

A fork in the path appeared and Moho skidded to a stop. He gestured to the left. "The heart of the lair is in there."

A lump swelled in my throat. Sulfur suffocated the air, lighting my lungs on fire with its thick poison. Without the oxygen sifting through the tunnels from the surface, we'd not be able to breathe at all. Within the cave shadows shifted against flickers of red. I squeezed Kupua's fingers. "Let's get this over with."

Kupua resisted my tug. "Wait." He stretched out his arm to Moho, palm up. "Take my hand, we must not get separated."

Sweat glistened on Moho's face and chest, mixing with the blood oozing from his wounds. Suspicion lingered in his eyes but he accepted Kupua's hand in his own. "Once inside, do not speak. Do not acknowledge the Lua Pele in any way, it gives the beast power."

"May the Creator protect us," I whispered.

Moho grunted. "Not likely."

Before I could protest, he slid into the cavern, yanking us along behind.

CHAPTER 24

TESSA

KAUA

BATTLE-PART I

Vapors of steam licked my skin with tongues of fire. Angry welts striped my arms and legs, like barbs of burning needles sinking into my soul. I felt a new appreciation for what Moho endured under the Lua Pele's control. Kupua's grip tightened and his touch focused my thoughts and flooded my mind with love. Red fog blocked our view and I shuddered to consider what else lurked in the chamber with us. Nobody had ever seen the Lua Pele. At least, not any that lived to talk about the experience. Silence hung in the air with a weight of its own as we strained for any sign of the monster we stalked.

Moho lurched forward and out of Kupua's grasp, lost to our sight with only his grunts to reveal his location. We surged into the thick mist, our arms stretched out as we blindly searched for him. Dropping to our hands and knees, our vision improved as the fog hung about twelve inches above the rocky floor. We spotted Moho, on his side with a black tentacle wrapped around his ankle. Another waved in the air, only instead of suctions on its ugly arm, circles of razor sharp teeth lined the undulating limb. He flung the spear above his head to block it as it slashed at his face.

Snatching my knife from its sheath on my thigh, I dove for Moho's leg and sliced into the tentacle holding him captive. Inky black blood mixed with the red pooling around Moho, but the slimy beast stubbornly clung to his flesh. The black substance burned my skin where it splattered, leaving more red welts blooming across my hands. Two more tentacles rose out of the fog like giant snakes without heads. I ducked as one swung past and Kupua pummeled the other with loose rocks and shards of bones.

Salty sweat beaded on my lip and slid down my face as I pried the chunk of severed limb off Moho's flesh. It wriggled in my grip, teeth grinding in search of more tender meat. I shuddered and tossed it as far from us as possible. The remaining tentacle withdrew in the dark as another took its place, curling and extending as it rolled toward us.

We all scrambled backwards until our backs slammed against the rock wall. It wasn't far enough. Moho stood with his weight on one leg, the other a shredded mess where the fangs of the beast had devoured him. I flung out my arm to block him from moving. "We need to retreat. You are wounded. We can return to this battle after you have healed but we can't fight this thing now."

"No. We end this now." He crouched, his shoulders flexed and with one good leg, he vaulted into the air, the spear poised for battle. He disappeared into the veil of steam and I held my breath. Blue and green lights flashed before an explosion erupted and a piercing ethereal scream rent the silence. A massive crack broke apart the floor and Kupua and I dove toward the cavern entrance, rolling away from the yawning gap.

CHAPTER 25

MOHO

KAUA

BATTLE-PART II

Tessa, Kupua and I retreated as far as the cavern allowed. The creature coiled under the cloak of vapors. Its voice snarled in my thoughts. *I will destroy your family. You will all die because of your betrayal. Today, I will feast on the flesh of your young.*

Pain anchored me to reality. My leg was shattered and unusable. It didn't matter. I had to finish what we had started. As I stood and steadied myself against the rock wall, another voice calmed me. The Creator. *I am with you. Together, we will defeat this evil. Give your trust to me.*

All doubts evaporated and I surrendered my will to the Creator. The one who had formed me in my mother's womb. The only one more powerful than the monster that waited for me in the darkness. Tessa spoke, but her words barely registered. I crouched, and lifted the spear into the air, swiping the jewel that ignited its force. A surge of adrenaline swept through my veins. The pain in my leg disappeared and was replaced by supernatural potency, blazing through every muscle in my body. I leapt into the unknown.

On the other side of the mist wall, a black, tangled, mass of tentacles spread out along the ground. The stench of rotted flesh and decay assaulted my senses. I landed and quickly sprang to a rock ledge above the deadly weave of flesh. Bones littered the rocks, reminding me how many had lost the battle I currently waged.

Your bones will be added to my collection today.

No pain accompanied the words. No fiery stabs of torn skin. The Creator whispered into my thoughts. *You are sheltered within my love. Evil no longer prevails in your soul.* Sudden confidence spread through my soul.

A sharp keening sound, like nails against a chalkboard captured my attention. I searched for the heart of the creature. Hidden in a depression of a grouping of rocks, the creature huddled. A round bulk of sickly gray cellulite with two round eyes, that seeped with blood red pus. Waves of undulating tentacles whipped around its body.

"I am yours no longer," I cried. With two strides, I reached my enemy and thrust the spear deep into one of its eyes. Flashes of blue erupted from the spear and spread through the creature like lightning. Its rubbery skin glowed as the brilliant beam expanded from within the beast, engulfing it in blinding blue light.

A tentacle struck my back, knocking me into the rocks. Toxic ink sprayed across my back, burning with the intensity of hot oil. The smell of sulfur invaded my nostrils and the ground rumbled, just before I slipped from consciousness.

CHAPTER 26

TESSA

LANAKILA

VICTORY

Kupua shoved me out of the cavern but I dug my heels into the sludge. "We can't leave Moho," I shouted above the chaos of the explosion.

"You go. I'll get him and be right behind."

"No, we stay together, remember?"

He exhaled and his shoulders slumped. "Fine. But please stay behind me."

He swiveled and scanned the cavern. Dust and smoke mingled to form a thick haze. Rocks continued to rain from the walls and ceiling. We maneuvered around boulders until we reached the edge of the crack in the floor, its width at least twenty feet across. "He must be on the other side," I shouted into his ear.

"It's too far to jump." Kupua crept to the wall and felt along the rocks with his hands. "This area feels stable, maybe I can climb across using the natural footholds."

My stomach dropped. "No, it's too slippery with all this steam. It's too dangerous."

He frowned at me, one eyebrow arched. "You doubt my mad climbing skills?"

"No. I doubt I could survive if you slipped into that hole."

His arms wrapped me in a sweaty hug. The scent of the sea that was Kupua, filled my senses and calmed my fears. He spoke into my ear. "Have some faith. I'll be fine. There's no other way to get to Moho, so it's climb or leave him and I'm not leaving him."

My body went limp in his embrace. "Okay. Just know that if you fall, I'm coming after you."

"Then I better not fall." He released me and gripped the rocks, wedging his fingers into the crevices and balancing one foot on a small ledge created by a broken boulder. With a flex of his muscles he heaved himself up, shifting his free foot into a nearby cleft in the wall. With each successful move, my heart fluttered until he leapt onto the far side of the cavern. I exhaled a sigh of relief and then he disappeared into the fog.

After several minutes, he reappeared and raised his voice across the divide. "He's alive, but injured. The beast is dead! He did it! There are a lot of bones over here. I'm going to try to use one as a bridge. Get ready to secure it on your side."

He vanished again and his grunts echoed in the space, letting me know something was happening. A thick, weathered bone, as large as a humpback whale poked from the haze and edged across the void. I stretched out my arms and grabbed hold, yanking it over and anchoring it with several rocks. With a sigh of frustration, I sat on the end just to be sure it didn't budge. Kupua helped Moho hobble to the edge and eased him to the ground before testing the bone with his foot.

"Please tell me you're not going to try to walk across."

"Moho can't walk. He's going to crawl across on his stomach. There's some rope over here so I'll tie it to his waist and toss it to you just in case. See if there is something you can anchor it with."

After securing Moho, Kupua threw the rope across the divide and I snatched it from the air. My fingers were raw and bloody as I looped it around the largest boulder I could find. Moho dragged himself to the bone and I eyed his effort with skepticism.

"I'm not sure this is a good idea. He's too wounded to have enough strength to get across."

Moho lifted his chin and glared at me. "I can hear you, Queen. I'm not dead yet. If I can vanquish that monster, I can do this."

Kupua shrugged. "We don't have much choice. This is the only way out."

I clenched the rope in between my palms and braced myself as I sat on the hefty bone and prayed to the Creator he'd make it across. "Ready."

With a heave of his arms, Moho inched over the abyss on his stomach, his damaged leg crossed over the other for stabilization. His arm muscles clenched and released as he tugged forward, one hand over the other. Halfway across he paused, panting with exhaustion. He reached forward and gripped the bone for another lurch forward. The makeshift bridge wobbled and his grasp faltered as his weight shifted off balance. His legs slipped over the edge and hung into the dark void. The rope tightened in my hands and I yanked it taut.

Kupua yelled encouragements from his side of the chasm. “Don’t give up, brother, you can do it. You’re halfway there.”

Moho grunted, the strain bulging veins on his neck and biceps. He hugged the bone while carefully positioning his good leg in the center, his damaged leg still dangling over the side like meat on a hook. He closed his eyes and clenched as he hefted it up and over the other, pain flickering in lines on his face. After another pause and several deep breaths, he inched forward again, closing the gap between us.

Once he was within reach, I abandoned my spot on the end of the bone and offered him my hand. “Take hold.”

He clung to my forearm as I lurched backwards and heaved him onto hard ground. For the first time, I noticed the scorch marks across his back.

“Thank you.” He murmured and rested his head on the rocky terrain, completely limp. A gray pallor tinted his skin and blood oozed from his tattered leg. The angry red welts checkering his chest and arms softened and faded, as did my own.

“You did it.” I gazed across the void and nodded at Kupua who winked and strode to the wall to return the way he had come. No need to trust in the stability of the bone bridge if we didn’t have to. I released Moho and scrambled to my side of the wall, holding my breath as his fingers dug into the crevices. He quickly crossed and pounced onto the ground, sweeping me into his arms and crushing me to his chest. “Kept my promise.”

My arms tightened around his waist, his sweat and scent filling my senses. Words caught in my throat and a trembling shook my limbs until the only thing keeping me upright was the strength of my love. "Let's go home."

He stroked my hair and kissed the top of my head. "Your best idea yet."

Moho couldn't be roused, his body limp and unconscious, face down in the rubble. Kupua squatted and pinched his wrist. "His pulse is slow, but strong. He's losing too much blood. We need to get him to Kele."

I ripped off a strip of my shirt and tied it around his thigh. "You take his arms, I'll grab his feet." We hefted Moho between us and shuffled through the tunnel. The temperature had dropped with the death of the Lua Pele. Cool air from the surface blew freely through the tunnels and dried the sweat on my face. My spirit lifted in joy. The Lua Pele was gone and with it the toxic odor of sulfur. We'd succeeded. I prayed Moho would survive to celebrate his victory.

CHAPTER 27

MOHO

HANAU

BIRTH

Pain shimmered through my awareness like a million sharp daggers clamping on my leg in a vice grip. Blackness cloaked my mind and only the pain anchored me to reality. My body refused to respond to attempts to move. Through the fog, a vision of plunging a spear into the eye of a monster filtered through. Was I dead? Had the Lua Pele claimed me for good? The scent of antiseptic stung my nose and if I concentrated I could make out murmurs of conversation. Not dead then.

You don't belong to the Lua Pele. You are free and one of mine, if you choose. Tendrils of comfort and peace sifted around me, erasing the pain of moments before.

"Creator? Why would you want me, after I've betrayed you, fought against you?"

I've always loved you and longed for your return. You are forgiven. Will you accept my forgiveness?

"I don't deserve it."

No, you don't. But I offer it and my love anyways. Do you accept?

Longing clawed at me. I wanted to accept but shame clung with the weight of a hundred lava rocks around my neck. "I am not worthy. Leave me to die."

There is work for you to do here in this world. Others who need you. Accept my forgiveness and start following the path I've forged for you.

Eka's face formed in my mind and hope strengthened me. For her and the baby I would make the effort. I had made her a promise. "I accept." The weight of shame immediately released its grip and I nearly floated in the cloud of love that embraced me. All the empty holes in my heart filled with joy, like a broken vase that had been re-formed into something indestructible and whole. However long I hung in the Creator's arms, it would never be enough. As the fog of His spirit lifted, I slipped into sleep, aware only of His healing presence.

Upon waking, I smelled garlic and antiseptic. My tongue stuck to the roof of my mouth and my lips cracked as I attempted to speak. A groan rumbled from my chest. A scurry of footsteps hurried in my direction.

"Brah, no move, da leg is brutal. Need surgery, but da baby come now, kay den. I get da surgery done aftah I deliver baby."

The baby? Awareness dawned. "Take me to Eka," I croaked, my voice cracking through what felt like a throat lined with rocks.

"You been all bus em up from da Lua Pele. Stay still brah and rest."

Power surged through my veins and I shoved myself off the pillow. Pain lanced through me sucking the air from my lungs. "No. I have to be there. Now."

His hand cupped my shoulder and pressed me against my pillow as he called over his shoulder. "Akalei."

Her face peered over me. "I'll roll his bed to the delivery room. You go take care of Eka."

My head plunked into the pillow. Kele's face disappeared from view. After a few clicks and bumps, the bed rolled down the hall.

"Now don't cause any trouble, big guy. We're all doing our best for both you and Eka. Promise me you won't try to get out of this bed."

I squinted through one eye at her. "No promises."

She huffed. "Isn't it about time to start trusting us, Moho?"

Trust. The word felt foreign, something I had no memory of experiencing. How does one learn something with no frame of reference? I decided not to respond, not worth my energy. Instead, I focused on enduring the agony that shot through my leg with every bump of the bed. Then I heard moans from somewhere close and recognized the voice. The bed swiveled until I caught view of Eka, propped up with pillows, hands on her knees, and face scrunched up in pain. Kele crouched at her feet.

"Move me closer," I shouted to Akalei, who gratefully complied. She scooted the bed next to Eka and I stretched out and snatched her hand. "Eka, I'm here. Are you okay?"

Her features relaxed and she slumped against the pillows. Exhaling a breath, she turned to face me, a faint smile brightening her face. "Moho. The baby is coming. This is so hard." Tears trickled down her cheeks, each one carving a river into my heart.

"You're doing great. Everything is going to be okay. Kele's a good doctor."

Kele grunted under his breath but I ignored him and wiped Eka's cheek with my finger. "I love you."

Her eyes twinkled in surprise. "Really?"

"Of course. We defeated the Lua Pele, I'm free now and will take care of you and the baby. I promise."

She squeezed my hand, then another surge of pain hit and she tensed. She screamed, panting as she focused on Kele's coaching.

"Da baby almost here. Push."

Red blotches bloomed on her face and chest. She gave it all she had and a torrent of emotions flooded me. Suddenly, her survival was all I could think of. "Help her, Kele. Do something!"

Akalei gently placed a hand on my shoulder. "This is normal. Eka will be okay."

"But she's in pain. Can't he do something to ease it?"

"It'll be over soon. Medicine wouldn't be good for the baby. Just be there for her. She needs your support."

Eka squeezed my hand and fell quiet again. I stroked her arm, feeling helpless.

"I can see da head. One push and dat should do it." Kele encouraged, his voice a low murmur stroking my panicked heart.

Sweat beaded on Eka's forehead, her curls plastered against her face. She swung her head side to side. "I can't. I'm too tired."

I slid my arm beneath her back. "Then use my strength. Let me help you."

She lurched upright as another contraction surged and leaned into my arm, allowing me to support her back as she focused on the push. A scream ripped from her lungs, this time joined by the cry from another, our child.

"It's a boy! A son." Kele used a cloth to clean the baby and then cut the cord. He swaddled the tiny bundle before handing him to Eka.

Eka accepted the child into her arms and twisted to her side so the baby nestled between us. Dark hair covered his head and perfectly formed fingers gripped into miniature fists. His cries quieted as we held him together, marveling at his golden skin and rosebud lips. "He's looks like you, Moho."

"No, he's too beautiful to look like me. He takes after his mother."

Her face glowed, as if lit within by a thousand candles. "You think I'm beautiful?"

Warmth burned in my chest until it couldn't be fully contained within my skin. "Stunningly beautiful. Eka, I'm sorry for not being the man you needed, for not being a good man. Can you forgive me?"

Tears swam in her round eyes, wetting her dark lashes. "Yes. Of course I forgive you." Her voice cracked and she dropped her gaze to our child. "We can be a real family now."

With my finger, I tilted her chin to look her in the eye. "I promise." Stretching across the gap in our beds, I pressed my lips gently against hers. The softness of her mouth melted like warm chocolate against mine. I would not fail Eka or my child. She'd believed in me when everyone else had given up and my heart swelled with gratitude. Eka, I could trust.

Kele cleared his throat from the end of our beds and pointed at my leg. "Eh! No get all salty but time fo' da surgery to fix da leg, brah."

"I don't think so. Eka needs me right now."

Kele's hands lifted into the air. "We cannah wait, da leg get all infected and den you in real trouble. I nevah let dat happen. Not on my watch."

Eka laid a hand on my arm. "Please, Moho. The baby and I are fine and we'll be here when the surgery is over."

"Are you sure you'll be okay?"

"Yeah, in fact I could use a little sleep."

I kissed her forehead and swung my gaze to Kele. "Fine, let's get this over with. But I want to wake up where I can see Eka."

CHAPTER 28

TESSA

HILINA'I

TRUST

"Keoni, God's gracious gift. It fits him." I cooed and rocked the tiny bundle in my arms next to Eka on the bed. Her cheeks flushed with pride.

"Moho named him. He wants to make the formal announcement to the city himself. Will you let him?"

"Do you believe he's really changed? Do you trust him?" I still had my doubts, even though I wanted to believe in the change I'd witnessed in him.

Her curls bounced as she nodded her head. "I've always trusted him so I may not be the right person to advise you. But I have faith in him, in who he has always been deep down inside that crusty, wounded exterior."

"We all hope Moho's heart is truly softened. I'll have to check with Kupua, but I think he'll agree that Moho hosting a naming ceremony is a step towards reconciliation. Will you stay and raise the baby here?" Silently, I prayed she wouldn't leave the safety and protection of our city. She'd been through so much already and most of it because of Moho.

She shrugged. "We haven't talked about it yet. As long as I'm with Moho, I don't care where we live. Keoni and I will go where Moho goes."

Little Keoni squirmed and fussed so I handed him back to his mother. His tiny fists gripped her hair as she tucked him against her shoulder. Hope warmed my chest. "Moku-ola will always be your home, no matter where you rest your head at night. We are family."

A smile played on her lips. "I know. Thank you for always being kind and accepting me, even when I didn't deserve it. I'm sorry for the trouble I've caused."

"Stop. We've all had our struggles and you've had more than your share. Love isn't earned, it's who we are. You will always be part of us here, just like Moho will always belong in this city as its prince, even if he doesn't believe the truth."

Her eyebrows scrunched together. "Moho never rejected you or his family, it's himself he's struggled to accept and forgive. Give him a chance, Tessa, and you'll see he's changed."

"I hope you're right." Nothing would make me happier than Moho being permanently restored to our family. Kupua had borne that loss for too long. I needed time to see if the change was sincere and lasted longer than his mood.

Akalei peeked into the room. "The surgery is over and everything went great. Kele will be wheeling the big guy in here in a few minutes. Don't want him waking up mad because he can't see you two." She pointed at Eka and the baby. "Can't say as I blame him, that little one is pretty adorable." She tip-toed over to Eka and leaned forward to gently kiss Keoni's cheek. He didn't stir, now fast asleep in his mother's arms.

Eka exhaled. "That's a relief. How long before he can walk?"

"Well, Kele says a week, but I'd bet Moho won't be a compliant patient."

"Can't argue with that logic," I responded. "That's my cue to get out of here and let you all rest." I glanced at Akalei. "You got a minute?"

"For my queen, always."

I rolled my eyes and waved her out the door. With a quick nod at Eka, I said, "I'll come back later to check on you, okay?"

She flicked her hand at me. "Don't worry about us. We're fine."

Easing the door closed, I edged closer to Akalei and lowered my voice. "Think you can put together a naming ceremony in a week?"

Her eyes sparkled. "Seriously? Have you met me?"

With a nudge of my shoulder against hers, I laughed. "Sorry, what was I thinking. I haven't talked to Kupua, yet and I'm still not convinced Moho will stick around, so keep it on the down low, okay?"

She winked. "I'm on it."

The jingle of wheels announced Moho's bed being guided toward Eka's room. Antiseptic lingered in the air around his still body as Kele glided the gurney past us. Even though he slept, his face glowed with a peace I had never witnessed on him before. The heavy lines normally carved beneath his eyes were softened and his mouth formed almost into a smile. I shooed Akalei farther down the hall. "Let's give them some privacy. I need to check in with Kupua and make sure he's okay with letting Moho host the naming ceremony for Keoni."

Kupua was easy to find. He sat with legs dangled over the edge of the palace main floor overlooking the sacred pool and center of our city. From this vantage point we could watch the daily pattern of our citizens going about their day. It was one of our favorite spots. Before I knelt to join him, he reached up a hand to clasp mine.

"How's Eka and the baby?"

"Right now they're doing great, but who knows what will happen once Moho wakes up. Do you believe this shift of his will stick?"

"I may not trust him but I do trust the Creator. It will stick."

I settled next to him and laid my head on his shoulder. His smooth skin warmed my cheek. "Eka wants him to host the naming ceremony."

He nodded. "Seems like the right thing to do."

"I thought you'd say that. Akalei's going to handle all the arrangements."

He squeezed my hand. "So why don't you sound happier?"

"If Moho is really back, I'll be ecstatic. It's just, if this doesn't last, I know what it will do to you, your mom and Eka."

"This isn't your burden to bear. If you don't trust Moho, at least trust the Creator…and me. I'm a big boy, and I know the risks."

The tight pain in my chest released a little and I inhaled deeply.

"Okay. I'll try to let it go."

"See that." He pointed to the sacred pool where Lizzy and Mimi floated lazily. Their slick brown bodies bobbed with the gentle waves in the water. Sid clung to Lizzy's head, his tentacles wrapped around her chin like the winter caps my sister and I used to wear when it snowed. "They've been waiting for you all day. They carry a message Sid insists must be delivered only to you." He rolled his eyes. "As if I couldn't be trusted."

I patted his shoulder. "Don't be upset with him. It's not personal. Sid takes his role very seriously. He's old school. You know, formal information must go directly to the Queen and all that."

He grunted. With one hand on his shoulder, I heaved myself to my feet. "Guess I better go find out what he has to say."

CHAPTER 29

TESSA

KAUMAHA

GRIEF

Sid released his grip on Lizzy and slid through the pool to wrap himself around my ankle as I dipped my feet into the pool. His tentacles flared out and curled around my skin like ribbons blowing in the breeze. The suckers tickled when he settled and his grasp on me tightened. His joy at seeing me caressed my senses and I stroked his sleek body with my fingers. "Good to see you, too, dear friend."

Sid's message flared in my mind, an urgent plea from an old ally. Sam desperately wanted news about his brother, Henry. My stomach churned. I'd forgotten about Sam in all the chaos and hadn't told him what had happened to Henry. How does anyone share the news your loved one is dead? My head sunk into my chest. I didn't want to do this. Lizzy nuzzled my leg, her whiskers tickling my skin. I scratched her chin and she splashed me with her flipper. Kupua must have noticed the change in mood as well. He gently touched my shoulder, tugging me from my thoughts. "Tessa, you okay?"

"I have to tell Sam what happened to Henry. How do I do that? It's going to crush him."

He eased to the ground next to me. "It's not your fault Henry's gone. He made his own choices."

"Yeah, but those choices are going to devastate a good man. Sam loved Henry just as much as you love Moho."

"You're right, but Sam has a right to closure. And, you don't have to do this alone. I'll be with you."

Lizzy barked. She wanted to go as well. "All right. Let's get it over with now so we can be back for Keoni's celebration."

Sam's home wasn't close. He lived on Catalina Island so we enlisted Fin's dolphin pod to get us there as quickly as possible. Once on the island, Kupua rented a jeep and we rumbled up the winding road to his estate. A light breeze tangled through my hair. Eucalyptus trees scented the air with their sweet perfume and shaded our path. Sweat broke out on my palms as I considered the words I would use to break the news. Every time the jeep lurched over a bump, my stomach flipped.

On both sides of the road, lay hillsides of grass being lazily grazed by the well-groomed horses Sam raised. Kupua turned into the driveway and eased to a stop. He shut off the engine and took my hand. "He already knows we bring bad news, otherwise we would not have come in person. Sam's smart and we owe him the truth about what happened."

I inhaled a deep gulp of fresh air. "That doesn't make this easy."

He stroked my cheek with his thumb. "No, the things that really matter are seldom easy."

With a last squeeze of his hand, I let it go and ejected myself from the jeep just as Sam emerged from the house. He looked older then I'd remembered with dark shadows under his eyes. Black stubble covered his chin and his clothing was rumpled and stained. I forced a smile as he opened his arms to welcome me with a hug, but I couldn't stop the tears filling my eyes. He smelled like unwashed laundry that had sat too long in the hamper. He held me tight against his chest and whispered into my ear. "I sensed he was gone."

Words choked my throat and only sobs escaped. Minutes passed and neither of us moved, as if doing so would somehow make the loss real. Sam loosened his grip first and I reluctantly followed. "Let's go out back where we can talk."

I nodded and followed him around the side of the house to the patio. Kupua looped his arm through mine and I leaned against him, grateful for his support. The smell of cut grass freshened the air and small birds chirped at us from the tree branches shading our path. We settled into iron lawn chairs with thick cushions decorated with palm trees. Sam handed us each a glass of water before directing his gaze to me. "Were you there when he died?"

My eyes shifted to Kupua. "No, I wasn't there. Kupua was the last to see him but Henry was alive when he escaped Moho. We can share what we've learned since that moment."

Sam zeroed in on Kupua. "I want to know how it happened and what his last moments were like. It's important. You have no idea the agony of not knowing."

Kupua scooted closer to Sam, his voice low and tinged with sorrow. "I didn't see it actually happen but I was there a moment before. It was an accident. Moho intended to sacrifice me to the Lua Pele and at the last moment he changed his mind. Something was shifting in his heart but the Lua Pele still had a grip on his soul. As I was leaving I could hear him and Henry arguing and then Henry was taken by the Lua Pele, into its lair. Part of me hoped when we attacked the beast we might find Henry alive. There was no sign of him. I'm so sorry."

Sam stared at his hands, rubbing one thumb over the other. Finally, without looking up he whispered, "Did you destroy it? Is it gone?"

"Yes. The Lua Pele will never take another life. Moho killed it."

"Good. Who's going to make sure Moho doesn't do anymore harm?"

Surprise flickered in Kupua's eyes before being replaced by a mask of calm. "He is in the Creator's hands now. He is forgiven, and if he stays on this path, he will rebuild his life with us."

Sam looked up and there was a hardness in his expression I hadn't seen before. "And what if he doesn't stay on this so called path?"

Kupua met his stare. "Revenge never heals the heart, Sam. Only forgiveness will give you peace."

"Forgiveness won't give my brother peace. His chance for redemption is gone, stolen. He's lost and nothing can bring him back. Where is the justice in that?" His head dropped into his hands and sobs racked his body.

I leapt from my seat and wrapped my arms around his shoulders. Words could not ease his grief so I just held him as his body shook.

Kupua's voice cracked. "We are so sorry for your loss, Sam."

"I think it might be best if you leave." His face remained cradled in his hands, his voice muffled with pain.

Releasing my arms from him, I stepped back from Sam and glanced at Kupua whose face wore the same stunned expression mine must have held. My heart tightened at the thought of leaving him in this condition. "Are you sure? We don't mind staying with you. This is hard news and it's not good to be alone. We're your friends, Sam."

At that he did look up. "But I am alone. He was my brother, my only family and now he is gone. I helped you, and your family has brought nothing but grief to mine. Now you tell me Moho will not be punished for what he has done. That is not acceptable and nothing you can say will make it better. Just leave."

Kupua stood. "We will respect your wishes but I want to make something clear before we go. Forgiveness for my brother does not mean there are no consequences for his bad behavior. There are consequences, although those may not be the punishment you seek. Revenge is never justice. He has suffered a great deal of pain and we believe our Creator is the one who dispenses his justice. Tessa and I are your friends and we will come if you need us. Peace to you, Sam."

Love swelled in my chest for my husband. The truth in his words settled over me in a mantle of warmth. I hoped they would soak into Sam and provide comfort. Leaning over, I kissed Sam's head. "Good-bye, Sam."

His body stilled but he did not respond. With a heavy heart, I accepted Kupua's outstretched hand and returned with him to the jeep.

CHAPTER 30

TESSA

MOHAI

SACRIFICE

Moku-ola welcomed us home with a quiet peace. A soft breeze blew through the tunnel, carrying the scent of salty ocean and cinnamon. Mimi glided into the water to greet Lizzy who clung to my side, one flipper hugging my thigh. Akalei sat cross-legged on the gravel beach, a lei of flowers draped in her lap. I crawled from the water and flopped down next to her as Kupua headed into the tunnel. She looped the lei around my neck and rested her head on my shoulder. "It's good to have you home, dear friend. I missed you."

"Missed you, too." I leaned my head against hers. Exhaustion tugged at me, weighing down every inch of my body until I wanted nothing more than to dissolve into my bed. "It didn't go well."

She patted my arm. "Give him time. Grief clouds the mind."

"Nothing more we can do for him. It's in the Creator's hands now." Her body tensed next to me. I shifted to face her directly. "How is everything here going? Is the ceremony on schedule for tomorrow?"

"We need to postpone it."

"Why?"

"Moho's leg is infected. Kele says it needs to be amputated, but has been waiting for you both to return before breaking the news."

"Moho doesn't know?"

"Kele thinks he suspects, but Moho is stubborn and keeps trying to push through the pain and walk, which is only making his condition worse."

"What about Eka?"

She shrugged. "Eka is supporting Moho and won't broach the subject."

Climbing to my feet, I sighed. "Guess we better catch up with Kupua and get this over with."

Kupua waited for us, his back against the massive door to our home, his eyes closed and face pale. As we approached, he straightened. "Why do you look like you have bad news for me?"

I sunk into his arms and pressed my face against his chest. "Your brother's leg is infected and Kele needs us to convince Moho to let him amputate in order to save his life. As much as I'd like to crash into bed, this can't wait. Duty calls."

The air left his lungs in a groan. He gave me a squeeze and spun us both to face the door. We positioned our hands on the smooth, carved wood and the locks released, opening into the entry of our home. We trudged straight to the healing rooms.

Kele met us outside the door to Moho's room, his face lit with relief when he saw us. "So glad you are here, brah! I want no beef wit dat Moho, but his leg is brutal. Gottah amputate today or it get mo infected. So sorry, brah. He nevah listen to me. It mo bettah if you talk to him."

Kupua grunted and pushed past Kele and into Moho's room with me trailing behind. Moho lay propped on a pile of pillows, cradling his son in his thick arms. Sweat beaded on his forehead and his face was tinted with a flush of red. Dark circles framed his eyes and he smelled of sickness. More pillows elevated his bad leg, which remained covered in seaweed bandages. Eka hovered nearby, worry etched across her features. Moho looked up briefly as we entered before concentrating again on the baby sleeping in his arms. "You think I can't hear you discussing me outside my own door?"

Kupua shrugged. "It's not a secret your leg is infected. You should know that better than anybody. Are you going to listen to Kele's medical advice or are you going to be difficult?"

Moho frowned and handed little Keoni to Eka. "My leg, my decision."

"I know this isn't easy, but if you don't let him take the leg, you could die. Do you want to leave your son without a father?"

Moho glanced at Eka who began pacing across the floor, shaking her head and rocking Keoni. He studied his hands for several moments before responding. "Is it really that bad?"

"Kele wouldn't suggest such an extreme measure if it wasn't absolutely necessary. If he thought you could save the leg and live, he'd be the first to try. You can trust him."

He grabbed Eka's wrist. "What do you think I should do?"

She froze and swallowed, slowly lifting her gaze to meet his. "Keoni and I need you. If keeping you alive means sacrificing a leg, it's an easy choice for me. I want you, with or without a leg. Agree to the surgery."

Releasing her wrist, he sighed and closed his eyes. "What good am I if I can't even walk? How will I take care of a family?"

Eka's voice rose. "Stop it. The Moho I know has more courage than this. You don't need two legs to swim or hunt in the ocean. You don't need two legs to love your family. And there are lots of options for when you are on dry land. Where is the bravery that helped you face off with the Lua Pele?"

Eka's mother bear had blossomed and her outburst made me smile. Even Moho seemed pleased with her response, the side of his mouth quirked up a bit before he shifted his gaze to Kupua. "Fine. I'll do the surgery. Go get Kele and let's get this over with."

CHAPTER 31

TESSA

LOKOMAIKA'I

GRACE

Lanterns swung from strands of shells suspended above the sacred pool. Their soft light flickered and cast shadows across the liquid surface. Moho's head and shoulders emerged from the still water as he balanced on Nikko's back. Ripples spread out around him causing small waves to lap against the sides of the pool. Water cascaded down his bare chest and his tattoo glistened. An uneasy truce had been reached to allow Nikko into the pool, much to Lizzy's dismay. She hovered on the edge of the water and growled under her breath. Small squirts of ink clouds gave evidence to Sid's anxiety at the presence of the massive shark we'd only known as an enemy.

A nervous hush pressed the small crowd as citizens of Moku-ola jockeyed for a better position to view the ceremony. Crates decorated with kelp kept the curious from sneaking too close and becoming a meal for Nikko.

The trail from the steps to the palace was roped off with garlands of flowers from the surface. Soft pink blossoms filled the air with floral scents. As Eka appeared at the top of the stairs, everyone stilled. Green chiffon draped over one of her shoulders and cascaded to her ankles, gathered at the waist with a belt of mother of pearl. Hiiakka followed Eka with Keoni cradled in her arms and joy beaming on her face. They carefully made their way down each step, one at a time, focused on their footing. When they finally reached the bottom, a sigh of relief escaped the crowd.

Eka's gaze lifted to Moho and locked on with an intensity that put the sun to shame. Her face lit with hope and expectation, shining as if an internal flame had ignited. Her pace quickened until she reached the edge of the sacred pool. They had decided to break tradition and conduct the ceremony in the water instead of from the glass platform above it. A naming ceremony held as much importance as a wedding in Moku-ola. It was a time when all the citizens pledged themselves to supporting the parents in raising up a child. As soon as Eka's foot broke the surface, a small blue shark rose to greet her and offer his back. She sucked in a breath before straightening her shoulders and lifting her leg over his side. Her dress bunched around her knees and ballooned in the water as she she reached to accept her son from Hiiaka. Little Keoni had fallen asleep, his lips sucking silently as he dreamed. She cradled him against her hip. The shark glided the short distance to Moho with her and the baby astride his back, stopping nose to nose with Nikko.

Moho's expression was somber. Kupua, Kele, Akalei, Hiiaka and I positioned ourselves on the edge of the pool and sat, dipping our feet into the warm water. Sid furled his tentacles around my ankle and peeked from the safety of my leg. He really hated sharks.

Moho's voice lifted into the air, loud enough all those gathered could hear. "I bear witness before you all that it is the Creator who has brought me to this place, forgiven me, transformed me and restored me to his care. I now ask Eka to forgive me for how I have wronged her." His eyes held Eka's, even as his voice wavered. A public apology was not something any of us had expected.

Eka lifted her voice, though it did not carry with the same force as she responded, "Who am I to withhold forgiveness the Creator has already given? Yes, I forgive you Ka-Moho-Ali and love you with all my heart."

His head dropped imperceptibly for a moment before he continued. "Eka is my wife and has taken her place as a member of the royal family. We exchanged our vows in private but now announce to you, with joy, that we are married." He reached below the surface and pulled a knife from a sheath on his leg. With a quick, clean cut, he slashed a line across his palm. "With your permission."

Eka's eyes widened as she nodded and he clutched her hand in his and carefully made a small slice in her palm. As blood bubbled from the small wound, Moho clasped their palms together. White light glowed around their hands like a pulsing orb. "With the Creator's blessing, in mixing our blood, I share my gift with you. You now share my control over the sharks. They will never harm you and will obey as you command. You are my partner and equal in every way. From here on, we work as a team, facing the adventure of life together."

Kupua and I exchanged a look. I whispered, "Did you know he could do that?"

His brows scrunched together. "It has not been done in centuries because there are risks. He must feel Eka needs the gift to protect her around the sharks."

Tears welled in Eka's eyes, but she made no attempt to wipe them. Instead, she sat taller and made her own pledge. "I promise to walk by your side with honor and share in your gift with integrity for the good of all in Moku-ola. Your responsibilities will be mine. No other but the Creator will take priority in my heart."

A smile broke on Moho's face and he tore his gaze from Eka's to look at the crowd. "In the name of the Creator, our union is sealed!" He turned back to her and leaned across Nikko's back to kiss her gently on the lips.

Moho stretched out his arms and Eka handed Keoni to him. A grin plastered Moho's face. He raised the child into the air and spun his shark in a circle before tucking Keoni into the crook of his arm. Astride Nikko, he faced the crowd and the happiness on his features slid into an intense seriousness.

"Good people of Moku-ola, I come to you forgiven by the Creator and asking for your forgiveness as well. For many years I have been your enemy and sought to destroy your queen and my brother. The Lua Pele held me in its thrall. That evil is now defeated and no longer holds sway over my heart. None of you will ever fall prey to its hunger again. It is my hope that I, and my family may start a new life with you. Will you accept me? Will you forgive me?"

Kupua's breath caught in the silence that followed, heavy with expectation. My own lungs tightened as we hung on his last words and waited for the response of our people. Kupua's fingers twined with mine. After several painful moments, Eka's cousin Jake stepped in front of those gathered. "On behalf of Eka's family, we declare our love for you, Ka-Moho-alii, and want all here to know you are forgiven and welcomed into our family. We offer you lokomaika'I, my brother. Grace."

Moho nodded at Jake before shifting his gaze back to the remaining throng. An older woman stepped up next to Jake, her chin lifted. "I have known you since you were born, Ka-Moho-ali, a beloved prince of Moku-ola and am overjoyed you have returned to us. Who are we to deny you the forgiveness already bestowed by our Creator?" She turned to face the crowd and raised her voice. "Do we not rejoice in this? Do we not shout with love and forgiveness that our prince is restored?"

A roar bellowed from the crowd, shouts of agreement from the mouths of all gathered. The ground vibrated as people jumped and pumped their fists in the air, exalting the goodness of the Creator who had returned their prince. A shiver went up my spine as I glanced at my Kupua whose face was wet with tears.

Moho's mask had also cracked and emotions stormed in his eyes. Eka had abandoned her shark and climbed on Nikko behind him, her arms wrapped around his middle and her chin on his shoulder. As excitement ebbed and the crowd calmed, Moho spoke with a wavering voice. "Words will not do justice to how I feel having received your love and forgiveness. Thank you. I will do everything in my power to repair what I have damaged. I vow to defend and protect all of you and our city here in the sea."

He lifted little Keoni above his head. "It is the great honor of Eka and I to introduce you to our son, Keoni, prince of Moku-ola. A son, born to the royal family, and dedicated by us to the Creator. Will you help raise up this next generation of servants to the sea?"

Cheers rose until I had to cover my ears to ease the pounding. A group of women carrying a basket brimming with gifts placed it on the edge of the pool before disappearing back into the throng. Kupua tugged on my hand and led me to the glass platform. We raised our joined hands into the air and waited for silence to fall.

"As Queen of Moku-ola, I acknowledge and welcome Prince Keoni into our family. Kupua and I vow to protect him and teach him the ways of caring for the sea. In accordance with our traditions, we present the first prince born to Ka-Moho-Ali, with a protector. A young dolphin has agreed to take on the role of ambassador for Keoni. Allow me to introduce you to Jet, the fastest young dolphin in his pod."

A flash of gray burst through the calm surface and flipped in the air before vanishing under the sea. Water exploded over all of us. Jet's snout popped out of the waves as he squealed and swam to where Keoni stirred in his father's arms. Jet nudged against the side of the great shark as if it held no threat to him and nuzzled little Keoni's dangling legs. The baby gurgled and cooed at the dolphin. Moho eyed the young dolphin with skepticism. He lifted his chin in my direction. "Eka and I thank you and accept this generous gift."

With a bow, I turned back to the crowd. "In honor of Keoni's birth, we have prepared a feast for everyone. Let us thank the Creator for this new blessing and celebrate our new family!"

As the attention shifted to platters of steaming rice and vegetables, Kupua and I knelt to assist both Moho and Eka onto the platform. Moho handed me his son before he clutched Kupua's hand and hoisted himself across the space between Nikko and hard ground. He lurched upright and balanced on his one good leg. Bandages wrapped the flesh below his knee. Eka pressed against his side and strapped an artificial limb fashioned from whale bone to his leg. "This will have to do until Kele gets one of those high tech devices from the surface."

He cupped her cheek and softly kissed her forehead. "Thank you."

A shiver shook me as my mind compared the Moho I'd first met to the man standing before me. The man who had once attempted to cut my throat on an abandoned ship. This was grace in action. Forgiveness when it was least deserved truly had the power to transform and our Creator had worked His grace on Ka-Moho-ali.

CHAPTER 32

TESSA

AMELIKA

UNITED

Late in the evening, Kupua and I strolled through a quiet city, listening to our footsteps squeak on the smooth polished walkway. Soft torchlight flickered to brighten our path and the scent of plumeria garlands hung in the air. We absorbed the peace coating our home following the night of celebration. Contentment blossomed in my chest with an expanding warmth that melted tension from every pore. Our family was united. Our kingdom was united. Finally, we could focus on our future. I rested my head against Kupua's shoulder. "Isn't it wonderful to have everyone we love together in the city?"

"Yes. It is. But you know Mike and Rachel will be leaving soon. They have to get back to the surface. Mike feels bad he's left his brother to handle the family store on his own for so long."

I sighed. "I'm going to miss having them so close."

"We'll visit them often. We've promised to help with Okalani, remember? And, now, we have Keoni to watch over."

"I know. There's so much I want to share with both those little cuties."

Two new lives added to our family. We reached the steps to the palace and paused to soak in the miracle of our lives. No more battles to fight. Our kingdom was at peace.

"What should be do first with all our free time?"

His hand slid down my arm shooting tingles through my stomach. His voice whispered into my hair, "How about nothing."

Another sigh escaped my lips. "Not sure I remember how to do nothing."

He shifted his arms around my waist, tugging me against his warm chest. The scent of sea and salt filled my senses as I breathed him in. He leaned closer until his nose brushed mine and his breath warmed my cheeks. "I'll help you remember."

ABOUT THE AUTHOR

Dr. Fairfield is a licensed psychologist with her doctorate from Northern Arizona University.

Tara grew up in Southern California and loves being near the ocean. Some of her fondest childhood memories are of swimming and snorkeling around Catalina Island. She has three grown children, three grandchildren and four dogs. Life is good!

When she's not writing, you'll find her having fun on the ocean, playing with her dogs or just hanging out with family in the Pacific Northwest.

Made in the USA
Middletown, DE
26 November 2017